Lila ran her fingers
were caressing Steven's
smile disappeared from her lips. The sweet, romantic words had changed, and she didn't like what they said.

> I can just imagine our future. We'll have a simple wedding in my parents' backyard. There'll be family and a few friends—only the people we care about the most. And we can have a cookout and pool party after the ceremony.
>
> Then, after spending our honeymoon kayaking and camping in the mountains, we'll settle down in a modest house with a porch swing and a white picket fence. It will have a few extra bedrooms, of course, for all the little Wakefields we'll have running around. The girls will have your beauty, and the boys will have my intelligence.
>
> Life will be one big family barbecue. And with my beautiful wife by my side—with you by my side, Lila—I know I'll be successful in the D.A.'s office. The pay will be next to nothing, but it will be enough to support us, although we'll have to give up certain comforts. . . .

Lila threw the letter back on the shelf and slammed her locker shut. *If that's what Steven has in mind for the future, he obviously has no idea who he's dealing with.*

Visit the Official Sweet Valley Web Site on the Internet at:

http://www.sweetvalley.com

FIGHT FIRE
WITH FIRE

Written by
Kate William

Created by
FRANCINE PASCAL

BANTAM BOOKS
NEW YORK • TORONTO • LONDON • SYDNEY • AUCKLAND

RL 6, age 12 and up

FIGHT FIRE WITH FIRE
A Bantam Book / January 1998

Sweet Valley High® *is a registered trademark of Francine Pascal.*
Conceived by Francine Pascal.
Produced by Daniel Weiss Associates, Inc.
33 West 17th Street
New York, NY 10011.
Cover photography by Michael Segal.

ISBN: 0-553-57071-4

Published simultaneously in the United States and Canada

Bantam Books are published by Bantam Books, a division of Bantam
Doubleday Dell Publishing Group, Inc. Its trademark, consisting of the
words "Bantam Books" and the portrayal of a rooster, is Registered in U.S.
Patent and Trademark Office and in other countries. Marca Registrada.
Bantam Books, 1540 Broadway, New York, New York 10036.

PRINTED IN THE UNITED STATES OF AMERICA

OPM   0 9 8 7 6 5 4 3 2 1

To Bari Paige Rosenow

Chapter 1

I can't believe this is happening to me, Lila Fowler thought, struggling to hold back a threatening flood of tears. She closed her deep brown eyes and prayed the events of the last hour were just parts of a bad dream. But the cold metal of the handcuffs clamped firmly around her wrists reminded her that the nightmare was all too real. She had been arrested and charged with arson.

As she was led into the police station and past the desk Lila kept her shoulders hunched and her head down, letting her long brown hair shield her face. She was painfully aware of the eyes that turned to stare as she walked by in her pale green satin dinner dress. Every so often she raised her hands to her neck nervously, intending to tug at the gold necklace she had purchased that afternoon. But the necklace was gone, along with her new emerald earrings. An officer had taken them from her and tossed them carelessly into a brown paper envelope.

I wish I could roll myself into a ball and disappear, she thought. *Then they couldn't stare at me with their accusing eyes.*

Her arresting officer, a tall, burly man with close-cropped brown hair, led her to a desk piled high with papers. Behind it sat a balding man in a short-sleeved polyester shirt. In spite of his pocket protector there were two ink stains seeping through the fabric.

Lila felt one corner of her mouth curling into a sneer as she looked at the smeared blue blotches. As soon as she realized what she was doing she wiped the grimace from her face. These officers thought she was a criminal. Who knew what they might do to her if she showed her contempt?

Gingerly Lila perched on the edge of a maroon vinyl-covered chair. The man barely looked at her as he started demanding information. In a monotonous voice Lila told him her name, date of birth, eye color, hair color, weight, and social security number while he scribbled furiously on a form. Then he asked her a question that turned her stomach.

"Have you ever been arrested before?"

Lila felt as if she'd been punched in the gut. Her mouth dropped open. "What?" she gasped.

The man stared at her and pushed his glasses up

on the bridge of his nose. His beady, ratlike eyes were watery and rimmed in red. When he spoke, he pronounced each word with exaggerated clarity, as if he were talking to someone who wasn't too bright.

"I—meant—have—you—ever—been—charged—with—a—crime . . . miss?"

"Certainly not!" Lila said indignantly. She jumped to her feet.

A corner of the man's mouth twisted into a smirk. "Don't get huffy, lady," he said. Then his expression turned to stone. His gray eyes bored into Lila's.

"Sit!" he snapped in a tone one would use to command a naughty dog. Lila felt color flame into her face as she did as she was told.

The man clasped his hands together on the desk. "This is a routine question, and I would appreciate it if you would simply answer it."

Lila drew in a shaky breath. "The answer is no," she said quietly. The man made a quick note on his form.

"We're through here," he said. He nodded to an officer, who took Lila by the shoulder and pulled her out of her seat.

What next? she whimpered internally.

Her latest captor had huge sweat stains on his uniform underneath his arms. Lila swallowed hard, choking back the urge to be sick.

Without a word the officer grabbed her hands and pressed her fingers one by one against an ink

3

pad and then onto a fingerprint card. Lila nearly squealed in pain each time he mashed another delicate fingertip against the white cardboard. *I guess this is what they call police brutality,* she thought.

Then came the pictures.

"Hold these numbers in front of you. Face forward . . . turn right . . . turn left." Lila Fowler was accustomed to giving orders, not taking them. From the moment she could talk, servants had scurried to fulfill her demands. Now she was the one being told what to do. And she wasn't even being treated in a civilized manner. She was being treated like a common criminal.

When Lila had officially been booked, a female officer with frizzy red hair guided her toward the holding cell.

"Let's go," the officer said wearily. She grabbed Lila as if she were a piece of meat at the supermarket. Lila thought the lack of expression in the woman's eyes was almost more frightening than anger would have been. Her legs felt rubbery as she passed by a cell full of huge, raucous women. One prisoner pulled up a tattered sleeve to show Lila a tattoo depicting a knife with blood dripping from the blade. Lila's eyes widened in horror as the woman laughed and blew her a kiss.

"Can't you tell I don't belong here?" Lila whimpered. The officer ignored her and kept a tight grip on Lila's arm, pulling her along. As they

4

turned a corner Lila stumbled. She had barely caught herself when the woman gave her a shove.

Lila stiffly walked a few more paces. Then the officer stopped in front of a dark, deserted cell.

The sound of keys rattling in the lock made Lila's heart pound. She broke out in a sweat all over her body as her breath came in short spasmatic bursts.

The officer leaned forward and unlocked Lila's handcuffs. Lila looked at the compact woman in disbelief. Was she letting her go?

"Step inside, miss," the officer instructed her.

Lila's heart dropped. For a moment she felt as if her whole body was frozen. *I can't go in there. Don't make me go in there,* a voice in her head pleaded silently. She was sure if she tried to take a step, she would faint.

"Step inside, miss," the officer repeated, a little louder and more firmly this time.

Somehow Lila dragged herself forward into the cell. She heard the clang of the door shutting and the keys rattling again, this time locking her inside. She whirled around to face the metal bars and saw the officer walking away.

"Wait!" Lila cried urgently. She rushed to the black bars and grabbed them with both hands. She yanked at them desperately, as if she could some-how pull them apart.

The officer turned. "What is it?"

Lila lifted her hands to the sides of her face. "You can't leave me here. I'm not a criminal!" she wailed.

The officer gazed back at her blankly. "I can't help you, miss. I'm just doing my job," she droned. Then she paused for a moment, her face softening slightly. "The best thing you can do is calm down and wait for the person you phoned to come and post bail. That's my advice. If you haven't done anything wrong, everything will be OK."

Then the officer was gone. As Lila looked after her a choking sob rose in her throat. She threw herself onto a rickety bunk and cradled her head in her hands.

The tears she had held back flowed freely now until her face was bathed in them. She thought she would never be able to stop crying again.

The idea that she had been arrested and charged with firebombing the Palomar House restaurant had thrown her into a state of disbelief and confusion. She curled up like a baby, bringing her knees to her chin.

How did those blasting caps and traces of fuel oil get into my car? she asked herself wildly. She had told the police she had never seen the junk before, but they'd acted as if they hadn't even heard her. *Why wouldn't they believe me?* She turned the question over again and again in her mind. How could anyone think that she, Lila Fowler, would even know how to build a bomb?

6

Lila wept silently as a feeling of total helplessness overcame her. Then, mercifully, she slept.

Jessica Wakefield and her twin sister, Elizabeth, glanced up at Adele, the District Attorney's receptionist. The middle-aged woman was usually full of cheery comments no matter how busy she was, but today she was eerily silent.

"I'm sure your brother will be ready to meet you for lunch soon," Adele said, running a hand over her silver-streaked, dark brown hair. She looked away and tapped her pen on the desk, seeming uncomfortable. "He and the D.A. are just having a little . . . discussion." She pursed her lips tightly and glanced at her watch.

"Oh! Look at the time!" Adele exclaimed, jumping up. "Well, I have some errands to run. So little time to get everything done on the lunch hour, you know." She grabbed her purse, nodded to Jessica and Elizabeth, and pushed through the office door. The sound of her high heels echoed in the hallway.

Jessica frowned as she turned to her sister. "Jeez. What's her deal?"

Elizabeth's eyes were clouded with concern. "She seemed preoccupied—like something was bothering her."

"Yeah, well, she couldn't wait to get away from

us," Jessica observed. "She was acting like we had cooties or bad hair or something."

Elizabeth smiled slightly. "Maybe it's just the workload," she said. "They've been working Steven to death."

"No kidding," Jessica muttered, rolling her eyes. "He spends so much time at this stupid office, you can hardly even tell he moved home."

Jessica was acting grumpy because she hated being made to wait, but she was actually excited that she and Elizabeth were meeting their brother for lunch. He was a prelaw student at Sweet Valley University and had a summer internship in the D.A.'s office. It was a great opportunity for him, but ever since he started, he had been swamped with the Fowler Crest arson case.

The cluttered office was a buzz of activity as usual. Interns and attorneys bustled to and fro between the cubicles, carrying files. Others sat hunched over computer keyboards or talked on the telephone.

As the minutes ticked by, the activity began to die down. The office staff started thinning out as everyone hurried to grab a quick lunch.

Jessica tapped her foot impatiently and tossed her long golden hair. "Come on, Steven, hurry up," she whispered, smoothing the hem of her trendy bright blue dress.

Jessica glanced at Elizabeth, who was drumming her fingers on the arm of the bench. For the umpteenth time Jessica wished she had tried to talk her sister into wearing something a little more hip than that plain navy blue dress with the little Peter Pan collar. Jessica bit her lip. *I should know better by now,* she thought. *Besides, if Liz wants to scare away any hot young lawyers who may be wandering around, that'll just leave more for me.*

Though the girls were identical twins, with the same silky blond hair, gorgeous blue-green eyes, and slender, athletic figures, they were also as different as two girls could be.

Jessica followed fashion closely and dressed in vibrant colors that reflected her live-for-the moment attitude and love of adventure. For her fun meant being cocaptain of Sweet Valley High's cheerleading squad, and she adored gossiping, shopping, and checking out guys. She firmly believed that once she got interested in someone, it was only a matter of time before she had him wrapped around her finger.

But Elizabeth's idea of fun was Jessica's idea of boring. Elizabeth loved reading, writing, and watching old movies with a few close friends. After school she worked at the *Oracle,* Sweet Valley High's newspaper, and hoped to become a professional writer someday. Her clothing tended toward wash-and-wear in muted tones and pastel colors.

9

Another important part of Elizabeth's life was her boyfriend, Todd Wilkins. Jessica thought Todd was more bland and tiresome than a biology film on the life of an amoeba. But with his tall build, broad shoulders, and deep brown eyes, even Jessica had to admit he was gorgeous. *But not half as gorgeous as* that *guy*, Jessica thought, admiring a blond, well-dressed intern who winked at her as he passed by.

Suddenly the door to the inner office opened and Jessica smiled brightly. She tapped her sister on the arm.

"Maybe that's Steven," she said excitedly. Then her face fell as the sound of angry voices filled the air.

She recognized Steven's strong, clear voice, now filled with notes of strain and tension. The other voice, with its low, gravelly tones, must belong to the D.A., she decided.

"Listen, Steven, I've told you again and again not to get personally involved with Lila Fowler. You were supposed to be investigating her, not starting a romance. This is the last straw."

Jessica heard the sound of papers being tossed on the desk. Then the D.A. continued. "If you post bail for her, you're finished here. You'll get no recommendation from me. In fact, if it were up to me, you'd be barred from studying to be a lawyer. As far as I'm concerned, you just don't have what it takes."

Jessica felt her jaw drop. She looked at Elizabeth

10

and saw her sister's eyes widen with surprise.

"I had no idea it had gone this far," Jessica whispered. "I didn't know they had actually *arrested* her." She crept closer to the D.A.'s office and waved her hand, motioning for Elizabeth to follow.

Through the glass panel on the partially open door Jessica saw the D.A., Joe Garrison, shaking his finger in her brother's face. The small, tough-looking man was clearly exasperated. He ran a hand over his short, dark curly hair.

"I'm telling you, Wakefield," he said. "I'm just about at the end of my rope."

Then Steven spoke, his tone respectful but his voice quaking with determination.

"I'm sorry you feel that way, sir," Steven began. "This internship means a lot to me. But I believe that being a good lawyer means standing up for your convictions, and I believe that Lila Fowler is innocent."

Steven's words rocked through Jessica. She knew how much the internship meant to him, and she felt a rush of pride that he would risk losing his job by standing up to the imposing D.A. She held her breath as she saw Garrison's face flush and a vein begin throbbing in his temple.

"She is the primary suspect," the D.A. said through clenched teeth. "Every bit of evidence points in her direction."

11

"It's all circumstantial," Steven said. "And if you'll just listen to me . . ."

"Don't you order me around, Wakefield!" Garrison bellowed. Jessica jumped slightly and saw Steven do the same. The D.A. took a deep breath before continuing. "I'm warning you, Steven, you're going to ruin your career as a lawyer before it has even begun." He shook his head, then looked Steven in the eye. "You will not bail the Fowler girl out of jail, and you will stop this silly infatuation once and for all," Garrison said evenly.

"And if I do bail her out?" Steven said, meeting the D.A.'s gaze.

"Then don't bother coming back here," Garrison replied.

Jessica gasped and covered her mouth with her hand. She glanced at Elizabeth, and her twin shot her a worried look. Suddenly Steven came charging through the door. His face was flushed, and his mouth was pressed in a thin line of determination. He did a double take when he saw Jessica and Elizabeth.

"Well, I see you've been eavesdropping, so you heard everything," he said. In a single, furious motion he loosened his tie, tore it off, and stuffed it in his pocket. "I'm going to post bail for Lila, and I don't want either of you to try to stop me." There was a cold glint in his eyes.

"Steven, calm down," Elizabeth said in a hushed voice. He ignored her. Then he got right in Jessica's face.

"You should have stood by her," he said angrily. "You were her best friend."

"B-But I *did* stand by her, Steven," Jessica sputtered. "I did everything I could to cheer her out of her depression after the fire."

"Yeah, *right*," Steven spat. "You're not even *talking* to her. How is that gonna cheer her up?"

Jessica pulled back as if she had been slapped. Steven hardly ever spoke sharply. She saw that Elizabeth's face had gone pale.

Jessica took a deep breath, drew herself up straighter, and put both hands on her hips. "Listen, Steven, I just couldn't stand by and let her steal my brother. You two are all wrong for each other, but you just can't see that. It's like she has some kind of spell on you." Suddenly she noticed the D.A. was watching them from the doorway, and she clapped her hand over her mouth again. Jessica's heart sank as she realized she had just confirmed all of the D.A.'s suspicions.

"I—I'm sorry, Steven," Jessica stammered.

Steven looked at the D.A. and then back at Jessica. An expression of disgust twisted his features. "It doesn't matter what either of you think," Steven said. "I am not going to desert Lila just when she needs me most. I'm not *you*, Jessica."

13

Jessica gasped and stared at Steven in disbelief. Why was he being so mean to her? She opened her mouth to reply, but her brother simply pushed past her and stormed out of the office, leaving his sisters in stunned silence.

Devon Whitelaw lay on his back, his hands clasped behind his head, looking out the window at the flickering neon sign.

"The Dunn-Inn Motel," he read in a whisper, and gave a short, humorless chuckle.

That pun certainly fits, he thought. *This place is definitely done in.* He pushed a lock of brown dark hair off his sweaty forehead and looked around at the cheap motel room, taking in the limp, frayed curtains; stained carpet; and dingy, peeling paint. *This room looks almost as lousy as I feel,* he told himself ruefully.

He returned to staring at the crack in the ceiling over the bed, something he had been doing for quite some time. The room had no air-conditioning and was so hot that his jeans and T-shirt stuck to his body. A trickle of sweat ran down his forehead and onto his cheek. He didn't bother wiping it away.

He didn't care about much of anything. Even his search for a home and family no longer interested him. He needed to find a legal guardian in order to receive his twenty-million-dollar inheritance. But

14

after all he'd been through, the money didn't seem so important anymore.

It was money that had caused all his problems. At the moment he was content to live without it. He decided he could live for five eternities, just passing his days in the anonymity of this room. At least he wouldn't have to deal with a bunch of users anymore.

Devon rubbed his hands over his eyes. *If it weren't for my father's will, I would never have ended up in this ridiculous place,* he thought.

"I wish I'd never left Connecticut," Devon told the empty room. Then he let out a rueful laugh. That was something he never thought he'd hear himself say. All his life his main goal was to get as far away from the East Coast and his so-called family as he could. And this dingy motel room in Death Valley certainly seemed a world away from the snobby Connecticut society he had lived in for so many years.

Devon sighed and thought back over the events of the last few weeks. Although it seemed as if an eternity had passed, it wasn't so long ago that he had stood in the foyer of his Connecticut mansion and heard the news that his parents had been killed in a car accident. Their deaths had been instantaneous.

From that moment the phone had rung off the hook. Cards and letters full of sympathy and emotion had poured in. But while the rest of the world had seemed to be mourning his loss, Devon had only felt numb.

His father, James Allan Whitelaw, had been a wealthy financier; his mother a professional socialite. Neither one of them had ever shown him much affection. Basically they had ignored their sole child, paying only the amount of attention required to control him. Devon supposed he was sorry they had died, but he couldn't say he missed them.

You can't miss what you haven't had, Devon thought bitterly. He never *had* felt like part of a family. And a family was what he had always wanted more than anything.

A few days after his parents' funeral Devon had left his Connecticut home in search of a guardian. *Not just a guardian,* he thought with a brief, stabbing pain of sadness. *Someone to be my family. Someone to really be there for me.*

The search had led him first to the home of his uncle Mark and aunt Peggy and his two cousins Ross and Allan. They lived in a modest split-level house in Ohio. It was a far cry from the lifestyle to which Devon had become accustomed, but it was the family's very normalcy that had given Devon comfort. Aunt Peggy and Uncle Mark seemed to be happy with the simple home they had created for themselves.

Devon got a bad taste in his mouth as he remembered how he had been taken in by his relatives.

16

Taken in and totally duped. They had pretended to care for him and welcomed him with open arms, but all along what they really welcomed was his money.

One night Devon had overheard his aunt and uncle talking and giggling about their plans for Devon's inheritance, plans that didn't include Devon at all. At that moment Devon's heart had hardened, and he knew what he had to do. He told Mark and Peggy that his parents had left him bankrupt, with nothing but the clothes on his back. Knowing they had already accrued a huge debt, Devon left them in the lurch, without a penny to repay their many loans. Devon knew it was vindictive, but he was also sure that his relatives had gotten what they deserved.

Next his search had led him to Las Vegas. He'd heard countless stories about his uncle Pete, who was renowned as the black sheep of the Whitelaw family. Devon figured that if normalcy had failed him in Ohio, maybe the complete opposite would serve him well.

"What a joke," Devon muttered, heaving himself off the bed and onto his feet. He paced the dingy room angrily.

I was so desperate for a family that I would have talked myself into anything, Devon thought. He kicked at a dust ball with the toe of his boot.

In his mind he had turned his uncle's rough edges into a harsh honesty he found appealing. And his uncle had said that he didn't care if Devon

17

had money or not because he didn't need any.

Devon's lip curled. That was the truth, he thought, though Devon hadn't found out exactly why Pete was so wealthy until later.

Next door someone turned a radio on full blast. It was a country-western station. "You left me with nothing but a bro-oken heart," wailed the singer.

Devon banged on the wall with his fist. "Turn that thing down!" he yelled.

The guy in the next room banged on the wall too, then cursed. But he lowered the volume.

How could I have been so desperate as to think I could spend my life in that tawdry, sleazy town? Devon wondered as he crossed the room and stared through the crusty window. *I was actually willing to plan a life spent in hotel rooms and casinos with a crook.*

Devon had finally found out his uncle was using him to deliver stolen merchandise to Pete's partner. She was a woman named Linda who helped Pete sell what he stole—diamond jewelry, gold lighters, designer watches—whatever he could get his hands on.

Devon smiled bitterly. All that time he had thought he was delivering gifts to Pete's girlfriend, when in fact he was unwittingly participating in a crime ring. Once he'd told Uncle Pete exactly what he thought of the way he made his money, Devon had gotten out of Vegas as quickly as possible.

Devon stuffed his hands into the pockets of his torn, faded jeans.

"What next?" he asked aloud. After all the pain he'd suffered, he felt as if he'd run out of steam.

Maybe I should just stay here, he thought, turning to look around the dilapidated room once again. *At least no one would be trying to get my money, or use me, or take advantage of me the way my dear old relatives did.* At least there were no lies in this lonely room. It was the perfect place for the guy who had everything, and yet nothing at all.

Chapter 2

As he drove through midday traffic in downtown Sweet Valley, Steven Wakefield's fingers gripped the steering wheel of his yellow Volkswagen so tightly, his knuckles shone bone white. The glare of sunshine on the streets was blinding. Steven's brown eyes, usually so calm and confident, squinted and flitted nervously from side to side. Sweat beaded his forehead.

Steven kept hearing the D.A.'s harsh, raspy voice telling him that if he bailed Lila out of jail, his internship—maybe even his career as a lawyer—was finished. The knot in his stomach twisted a little tighter.

Am I doing the right thing? Steven wondered.

He had to admit there was a lot of evidence pointing to Lila's guilt. After the fire at the Fowler Crest mansion, a hospital worker had found traces of sulfur on Lila's fingers. They had also discovered a book of matches in her pocket and an empty gas can in the back of her car. Later, Steven himself had uncovered an extremely incriminating piece of evidence—gas-soaked gloves, monogrammed with Lila's initials, hidden in the bushes in front of her house. Those powerful clues were hard to ignore.

Steven knitted his brow. Although the D.A. was convinced that Lila was the prime suspect, Steven couldn't come up with a good reason why she would want to destroy her own house. There had been tears in her eyes when she had described seeing her magnificent mansion in ruins.

Steven didn't think Lila would firebomb a restaurant either. True, she had been away from the table when the bomb had come crashing through the window, but he didn't think she had been gone long enough to execute the crime. Plus the entire dining room had been instantly engulfed in flames. It was a miracle someone hadn't been seriously hurt—even killed. He didn't believe Lila was capable of doing something that would put people in danger. She was too sweet and intelligent. Plus even if she *was* guilty, she would never be stupid enough to leave bomb paraphernalia in her car at the scene of the crime.

Steven stepped down on the accelerator and shot through a space between a brown Toyota and a blue Lincoln into the next lane. *I've got to get to the station fast*, he thought. He couldn't bear to think of Lila in a jail cell. He felt hollow inside just imagining how frightened and confused she must be over the arrest. The experience of being behind bars was probably driving her to despair. The only reason he had waited *this* long was because he had known the D.A. was going to be angry with him, and he had wanted to explain his reasoning for bailing Lila out in person.

Suddenly the guy he had just cut off leaned his head out the window of his brown Toyota. "Jerk!" he shouted. Steven twisted around and got a glimpse of his chubby face, reddened with anger. "Why don't you learn to drive?" the man yelled.

Steven glanced in his rearview mirror. "Sorry, man," he whispered. "I've got more important things on my mind." *Things like getting my girlfriend out of jail and clearing her name.* He ran his finger nervously under his collar.

Lila had seemed so fragile and alone when they forced her into the squad car. Her beautiful hair had been disheveled, and her eyes had looked panicked. She had reminded him of a frightened little girl.

Steven raked a hand through his brown hair. He remembered the many times she had told him that she needed him. Much as he had tried to keep their relationship all business, her fragile vulnerability had combined with her exquisite beauty to tug at his heart. Soon he had found himself thinking about her more and more—and not just as a suspect or as one of his sister's friends.

The brown Toyota swerved in front of him. The driver shot Steven a superior smile as he passed. Steven barely noticed. He didn't hear the horns honking at him either. He was lost in thought.

Suddenly the image of the computer printout someone had dropped anonymously into his in box appeared in his mind's eye. It had listed common characteristics of arsonists: Someone who needs affection and excitement. Someone who is crying out for help and attention. In the weeks Steven had been dating Lila, he'd found that those qualities fit her perfectly.

There was another item on the list that fit Lila as well—at least partially. She seemed to be fascinated by fire. She collected souvenir matchbooks from restaurants, and a mesmerized look came over her beautiful face whenever she stared into a candle flame.

Do I really know her as well as I think I do? Steven asked himself.

Distractedly he steered the Volkswagen into the next lane and made a left-hand turn. The Web page had turned out to be more trouble than it was worth. It had been the subject of one of Steven's first arguments with the D.A.

The printout had been slanted at an odd angle. He had seen the same slanted lines on pages that came from John Pfeifer's printer at the *Oracle* office.

Steven had been sure that this evidence proved that John had burned down Fowler Crest and tried to implicate Lila by leaving the Web page on Steven's desk. The D.A. hadn't agreed with his theory. In fact, he had practically thrown Steven out of his office.

Steven gritted his teeth. He knew he was right about this. Pfeifer certainly had the motive. Some time ago Lila had told everyone that John had attempted to rape her, and another girl had come forward with a similar story of her own. Although neither girl had brought formal charges against him, John had become an outcast at Sweet Valley High. Even Elizabeth avoided being alone with him in the newspaper office.

An exceptionally sharp blast of a horn started Steven out of his thoughts. He looked into his rearview mirror and saw a blue sedan close on his tail. At first he was annoyed, but then a quick check of the speedometer showed that he had slowed way below the speed limit.

Steven stepped on the gas. He told himself he'd better stop daydreaming and pay attention to the road, but he found his mind wandering once more.

Elizabeth and Lila had both confirmed that ever since Lila had confronted John about the attempted rape, he had hated her. Steven thought John had gotten off much too easily. He should have been prosecuted.

But now, it seemed, it would be Lila who would

24

face prosecution. Steven still thought all the evidence against her was circumstantial, but even he had to admit, the situation was looking more and more bleak.

This last incident—the firebombing of the Palomar House restaurant—was particularly disturbing.

The fact that she wasn't in the dining room when the bombing occurred made things look bad enough for Lila. But then the police had found an empty can of nitrate fertilizer in her car, along with traces of fuel oil in the upholstery and a torn label from a box of blasting caps. It was all basic home-made firebomb material. As far as the police were concerned, that evidence sealed Lila's guilt.

But that stuff could have been planted, Steven thought. He decided he'd have to question Lila some more. So far all he really had to go on was his belief that Lila was too scared about everything that had happened for her to be guilty. It was enough to convince him of her innocence, but he'd have to come up with more to convince anyone else—especially the D.A.

The car up ahead was looming too close, and Steven jolted back to reality. It was the brown Toyota. He jammed on the brakes, and they caught with a sickening squeal. He shot forward until his forehead nearly touched the windshield. Then the seat belt yanked him backward. He slammed against the seat with a thud.

"Moron!" the guy behind him yelled. "You're going to get someone killed. Get off the road!"

Steven took a deep breath and let it out slowly. "Get a grip, Wakefield," he muttered.

He turned the wheel and eased out of traffic. As he pulled into a space at the curb his heart was pounding and his hands were cold and clammy.

Steven leaned his head against the leather cover on the steering wheel and took several deep breaths. After a few moments he sat back in his seat. He felt sick to his stomach.

Am I doing the right thing? the nagging voice in his head asked again.

Yes, he answered silently. *I still think Lila was set up.*

"What if I'm wrong?" he asked himself, wiping his brow with his sleeve. "What if I'm just too stubborn to face facts?"

An image of Lila's beautiful face appeared in his mind. He remembered how perfect life seemed when he held her in his arms and felt the gentle pressure of her lips as she returned his kiss. Her silken hair was so soft and smelled so sweet.

He turned the ignition and carefully pulled back onto the street, turning in the direction of the police station. As he drove away he remembered John Pfeifer's words when he had warned Steven to stay away from Lila: "She destroys everyone who cares about her."

Steven shook his head. In spite of John's warning

26

he knew it was his own fault he had lost the job, not Lila's. If he had it to do over again, he would still stand up for his principles. He knew that he could prove without a doubt that Lila was innocent.

He had to.

Or Lila might be locked away for a long, long time.

Elizabeth dropped her slice of pizza back on her plate and sighed.

"What's the matter, Lizzie?" Jessica asked, taking a huge bite out of her own slice and washing it down with a sip of soda. "Aren't you hungry?"

"I don't know how you can eat after that scene with Steven back at the D.A.'s office," Elizabeth said, reaching for her glass of water.

"How can you *not* eat?" Jessica answered. "A good fight always makes me hungry. And Guido's pizza is perfect for a pick-me-up."

Elizabeth rolled her eyes and looked around the familiar restaurant. The atmosphere was upbeat and social as different groups of SVH students crammed into booths and greeted friends. But even though Jessica and the rest of the world seemed to be perfectly happy, Elizabeth couldn't force herself to crack a smile. She had this overwhelming feeling that Steven was headed for a major disaster.

Jessica popped a last bit of pizza crust into her mouth. "Come on, Liz," she said after she swallowed. "You have to break out of this funk."

"I just think Steven's taking a terrible risk by bailing Lila out of jail." Elizabeth crossed her arms over her chest and sat back in her chair. "I know it sounds terrible—but I still think it's possible that Lila is guilty." She held up her hand like a stop sign when she saw her sister open her mouth to protest.

"Wait a minute and hear me out. I know Lila's your best friend. . . ."

"*Was* my best friend," Jessica grumbled.

"Was," Elizabeth amended, "until the two of you fought about her seeing Steven. And the idea that someone we've known practically forever could be an arsonist is pretty far-fetched. But people can surprise you."

"Look, Liz," Jessica said, leaning forward. "I might think Lila's insane for dating someone as completely wrong for her as Steven, but I don't think she's psycho enough to burn her own house down. I mean *come on.* Do you really think she'd put her designer wardrobe at risk? Let alone all her fabulous jewelry and her private screening room and—"

"Think about it," Elizabeth interrupted. "Every time some criminal is caught, there are always a bunch of people who come out and say they never would have thought that person was capable of the crime."

Jessica's face twisted into an exaggerated grimace of disbelief. "Liz, you're being ridiculous!"

she cried. "Lila isn't an arsonist. She's a good person. Well, at least *most* of the time."

She crumpled up her napkin and threw it down on the table. Her lips curved down into a frown. "Lila isn't guilty of anything more than stealing our brother."

Elizabeth used a straw to poke at a piece of ice in her glass. She should have known Jessica would blindly defend Lila. She didn't want to believe her sister's lifelong friend would commit such a heinous act either, but there was a ton of evidence against her. And Elizabeth had never been one to ignore the facts.

"Whether she's guilty or not," Elizabeth said after a moment, "I don't like the fact that Steven's gotten mixed up in all this."

"I know," Jessica said, grabbing another slice of pizza from the pie in the middle of the table. "I don't think I've ever seen him so mad. I keep thinking that if one of our schemes to break them up had worked, he would at least be acting rational."

"And now even jail can't keep Lila and Steven apart," Elizabeth muttered. "He's gone down there to bail her out—and ruin his career in the process, I might add."

Jessica tossed her hair. "Well, even though I'm sure those two shouldn't be together, I'm *proud* of Steven for standing up for what he believes in. He thought he had to help Lila, and he refused to back down."

"That's true," Elizabeth agreed with a small

smile. "It was kind of cool the way he stood up to that jerk Garrison." She let out a long sigh. "But when I think of Steven and Lila wrapped in each other's arms the way they were that day in the kitchen . . ." Her voice trailed off.

"I just get sick," Jessica finished for her. Then she shrugged. "You know I don't usually give up easily, but it seems like we've done everything we could. I've tried talking to Lila about Steven and making him sound as repulsive as possible, but she just doesn't want to hear it."

"And Steven won't listen to reason either." Elizabeth picked at a piece of pepperoni. "But maybe we haven't tried hard enough. I wish he could see how perfect he and Billie were for each other."

Elizabeth had adored Steven's ex-girlfriend, Billie Winkler, with her beautiful chestnut hair and glowing smile. Anyone could see how in love Billie was with Steven. They both had the same simple tastes too. Billie was happy with barbecues, baseball games, and going out for spaghetti, just like Steven.

The two of them attended Sweet Valley University and lived together in a little apartment off campus. Everything was going so well between them. Then Steven told Billie he would be back home all semester, interning in the D.A.'s office. Billie had felt hurt—left out of Steven's decision. She thought he had chosen work over her, and the two of them had split up.

Elizabeth twisted a piece of silky blond hair between her fingers. "That stupid breakup could have been fixed right away. And I bet Steven could *still* get Billie back too."

"Except that now Lila has her hooks into him," Jessica said with a scowl.

Elizabeth sat up straight. "Well, there has to be some way to get those hooks *out*," she said. "Even if Lila isn't guilty of arson, she would still make Steven's life miserable. Imagine what his future would be like with her. . . ." She closed her eyes and began to paint the picture for Jessica.

"Steven works day and night to get Lila everything *she* wants and nothing *he* wants. She keeps pushing him harder and harder." Elizabeth leaned forward and spread her hands flat on the table. "Then when he comes home and wants to kick back and relax, Lila makes him take her out to dinner . . ."

"And not for something simple like tacos or fried chicken that Steven would enjoy," Jessica contributed. "*Oh, no.* They'd have to get all dressed up and go out to some fancy place that costs about a zillion dollars, where every dish on the menu has some unpronounceable name."

Elizabeth opened her eyes and smiled her agreement at Jessica before continuing.

"On weekends when Steven wants to go to the

31

movies or to the beach, he won't be able to—because Lila will throw long, boring parties where only the 'right' people are invited. She'll nag Steven to stand around in a dinner jacket, kissing up to people who can improve his career."

"Meanwhile," Jessica added, "Lila will be getting her hair done, getting her nails done, hiring servants, talking to interior decorators, going shopping, and spending lots of money. Plus she won't even let Steven buy a dog because she won't allow a little mutt to shed on her fancy furniture."

"Oh, no," Elizabeth said with a grin. "Only hairless cats for Ms. Fowler-Wakefield."

"Ugh!" Jessica groaned, holding her stomach as if she were about to be sick.

"So here's the deal," Elizabeth said, resting her elbows on the table. "We have to come up with something over the top. So far we've been practical and subtle, and it hasn't worked."

"Right," Jessica agreed with a sharp nod. "It's time to take some serious action." A slow smile started to spread across Jessica's face. "Wait a minute . . ."

Elizabeth felt a tingle of curiosity and anticipation. She could almost see the wheels turning in Jessica's head. Count on her conniving twin to come through with a devious plan.

Suddenly Jessica's face brightened as if a lightbulb had switched on inside her head. "That's it!"

she said, snapping her fingers. "The one thing Lila and Steven have in common is their stubbornness. They won't listen when *we* tell them they're totally incompatible, so we have to try something else." She tapped her fingers on the table.

"Like what?" Elizabeth asked.

"We just have to find a way to make them see it for themselves." Her eyes danced as she gazed across the table at Elizabeth. "And I think I know just how to do it."

Lila perched on the edge of the thin mattress and twisted her fingers nervously. *Hurry up, Steven,* she urged silently. She looked up at bars on the tiny window above her and felt a wave of panic threatening. With each passing moment she became a little bit more restless and a lot more scared.

She had woken earlier to find herself still locked in the cramped cell. Lila longed for the splendor of the Fowler Crest mansion. Her family's twenty-room Spanish-style home boasted a genuine crystal chandelier in the foyer and an Olympic-size swimming pool in the back. Priceless paintings by world-renowned artists hung in every room. *But that was before the fire,* Lila remembered.

Lila felt a lump rise in her throat as she leaned forward and rested her elbows on her knees. She knew that she had been under suspicion of arson ever since that awful night—the night much of her beautiful home had burned to the ground.

Whoever set fire to her house had also bombed the Palomar House last night—she was certain of it. And she knew that both fires had been set to make her look like the guilty party. They were acts of cruel, twisted vengeance. For the millionth time Lila wondered who could hate her enough to take away her home and almost take her life.

At least my parents weren't there. Lila sighed. *If they had been in their room, they would never have gotten out alive.*

My parents, she thought bitterly. George and Grace Fowler were separated when Lila was very young, but they had recently been reunited. When she was a little girl, Lila had always wished for a family. But now that her wish had come true, her parents were never around. They had been on several so-called second honeymoons since they remarried.

A few weeks ago her parents had been flown via private jet to a remote island in the South Pacific. They weren't even reachable by phone.

If they really cared, they would have made sure there was a way for me to get in touch with them, Lila thought bitterly.

Lila stood, tiptoed toward the small window, and gazed out, wondering if she was ever going to get out of this tiny, suffocating space.

"Steven," she whispered. "Where are you?"

She had been on a date with Steven Wakefield when the police had arrested her. As she was dragged toward the squad car he had promised to help her. *But that was last night,* Lila thought. *Maybe he isn't coming for me. Maybe he thinks I'm guilty.*

Quickly she banished the thought from her mind. He couldn't possibly think that when she left the table to go to the ladies' room, she had actually gone outside, constructed a bomb, and hurled it through the restaurant window. He was much too intelligent for that. And Lila knew he believed in her innocence.

Steven had been her knight in shining armor from the moment she had woken up in the hospital after the fire that had destroyed her home. She had felt so alone and frightened, but then she had found herself staring into a pair of kind, deep brown eyes.

When she'd realized it was Steven Wakefield, she had been disappointed at first. She'd always thought of Steven as her best friend Jessica's ordinary, boring brother with the silly sense of humor and bad wardrobe. But all that had changed. He had become her rock of strength and her hero all rolled into one.

Sometimes the strength of her feelings for Steven overwhelmed her. She thought their future was full of possibilities. In spite of everything Jessica said to the contrary, she was sure that she and Steven were the perfect couple.

My dear Steven, Lila thought as a silent tear rolled down her cheek. She longed to feel his arms around her. *He's the only one who believes me,* she thought. *He's the only one who can help me prove that the charge of arson is false.*

A loud clang sounded from the direction of the police station offices and Lila spun around, her heart in her throat. She heard hurried footsteps and hushed voices. Lila strained to hear whether Steven's voice was among them.

Then, like a vision, she saw Steven's strong figure coming down the hall toward her cell. The same frizzy-haired female officer who had locked Lila in was with him.

Lila's heart leapt in her chest. "Steven!" she cried, running up to the bars. "I thought you'd never get here. It seems like I've been in this place forever."

She stared into his kind eyes and feared she might sob with relief.

"I know, I know," he said soothingly. "You'll be out soon. They're just finishing up the paperwork. I have to wait out front, but don't worry. It'll only be a few minutes."

Lila reached through the bars and clutched Steven's hand. "Please don't leave me in here alone again. I don't think I could stand it." She heard her own frightened, little whiny voice and was immediately disgusted with herself. But she couldn't help it. She *had* to get out of this cell.

Steven lifted her hand and kissed it, then clasped it firmly, reassuringly. "I have to go, Lila," he said quietly. "If I don't go out front, I can't sign the papers. It won't be long. I promise."

A single tear squeezed from Lila's eye, and she felt her bottom lip start to quiver. Out of the corner of her eye Lila saw the officer fold her arms and shake her head in disgust.

Lila took a deep breath and lifted her chin defiantly. "All right, Steven, go ahead. I was just a little rattled, that's all."

"Good for you." Steven gave her a wink. "I'll be right back." And with a nod he was gone, leaving Lila totally alone once more.

Ten minutes later the frizzy-haired officer unlocked the door of Lila's cell.

"Looks like you got lucky," she said.

As if being arrested and thrown in jail could possibly be lucky, Lila wanted to snap. But she held her tongue. She didn't want to do anything that might keep her in this horrible place even one second longer than she had to be.

"So long, honey. Congratulations on getting outta this dump," the woman with the tattooed arm called. Lila shuddered.

Her heart pounded with impatience as she went through the process of completing the paperwork and retrieving her jewelry and purse. She hated the fact that so many hands had touched her things.

Steven led Lila out of the police station, and the minute the door closed behind them, she flung herself into his arms.

"I knew you'd rescue me," she murmured, burying her face in his shirt. His strong arms wrapped around her tenderly.

Lila reached up and ran her fingers through his hair. "You make me feel so safe," she whispered.

Steven kissed her forehead gently. "Don't worry, Lila. Everything will be all right," he murmured. "We'll get through this together. I'll prove you're innocent." He slipped his hand underneath her hair, massaging her neck softly.

"Oh, Steven." Lila gave a low purr of pleasure. She closed her eyes and leaned against him. For a moment she almost forgot the awful situation that had taken hold of her life.

Finally she pulled back and smiled up at him. "I want you to take me straight to the Silver Door," she said, giving her body a little shake. "I want to spend some time in the Jacuzzi and then have a massage and maybe a seaweed wrap. Then I'll just lie back, sip a glass of cold, delicious, sparkling spring water, and relax for the rest of the day."

"Are you sure you want to go straight to the salon?" Steven asked. "I mean, I thought . . ."

Lila looked down at her clothes and gasped.

"Oh, my gosh! Steven, you're right," she said. "I must look ridiculous wearing this cocktail dress in the middle of the day. The people at the salon would probably laugh me right out of there. Maybe I should go home and change first. . . ."

She stopped suddenly and studied Steven's face. He was staring at her intently, and his eyes were wide with confusion.

"What's wrong?" she asked.

Steven hesitated. "I thought you'd want to spend some time with me. You know, just the two of us. I thought we could go over the case a little more. We could go get a cup of coffee. . . ."

Lila's eyes narrowed. She had just had the most horrible, disgusting, undignified experience of her entire life and Steven wanted her to sit around drinking *coffee?* Not likely.

"Steven," Lila said, trying to keep her voice calm. "I don't want to talk about the case anymore. I've already told you everything I know."

"OK," Steven agreed, taking her by the arm and leading her toward his car. "We don't have to talk about the case. But let's at least go get something to eat together. . . ."

39

Lila turned to face Steven as he opened the car door for her.

"Listen, Steven," Lila said impatiently. "I just want to go home, get changed, and go to the salon. If you don't want to take me, I'll drive myself."

"I don't understand." Steven looked perturbed. "I just thought you'd want to spend some time with me after being alone in that cell all night."

Lila softened a bit at the little-lost-boy expression on his face.

"Of course I want to spend time with you," she said, leaning over to give him a peck on the cheek. Then she plopped into the passenger seat and slammed the door. "Just not right now."

Chapter 3

Devon was back in position, contemplating the crack in the ceiling, when there was a rap on the door of his motel room.

The bedsprings creaked in protest as Devon hauled himself to his feet. He opened the door and shut his eyes tight for a moment against the wave of bright sunshine that flooded the room.

"Mail!" an unusually loud voice announced.

"Thanks." Devon opened his eyes and accepted the stack of envelopes that was thrust toward him. He glanced at the desk clerk. He was a skinny, stoop-shouldered fellow in his late forties with pockmarked skin and thick, black-framed glasses. Instead of turning away, the clerk kept standing there, wearing a bewildered expression.

"Oh," Devon said after a moment. "I get it. You want a tip." He fished in the pocket of his jeans and handed the guy a dollar. The clerk accepted it without a word and shuffled away.

Everybody's got their hand out, Devon thought sourly as he closed the door. He sat on the edge of his bed and rifled through the envelopes, examining the return addresses: Connecticut Department of Taxation and Finance; Law Firm of Boyd, Dewey, Cheetam, and Howe; Egress Funeral Home; Havermeyer Landscaping. . . .

All legal stuff and bills, Devon realized. He rapped the mail against his palm and then tossed the entire stack into the wastebasket.

Why should I care about all that stuff? he wondered. *It's all part of my past.*

After a moment Devon sighed with resignation and fished the stack of mail out of the wastebasket. It wasn't as if he had anything better to do.

Devon thumbed through the stack until he came across a small, white envelope. It was addressed in neat handwriting rather than a computer-generated label like the rest of the mail. Devon read the name and address—Nan Johnstone, Thirteen Hummingbird Lane, Sweet Valley, California. Nan Johnstone. Why did that sound so familiar?

Then in a rush it came back to him, and he almost dropped the envelope. Nana!

Warm feelings flooded through him as he recalled the woman who had been his childhood nanny. With her sweet face and auburn hair pinned on top of her head, she had seemed like an angel. He recalled Nana smiling at him as she pulled a tray of cookies from the oven, Nana holding him up to see the puppies in a pet store window. For years Nana had dried his tears and bandaged his skinned knees, and then . . .

Devon's throat closed, and he felt as if someone had drenched him with an icy bath. The happy recollections were replaced with a memory of the day at age seven when he had stood in the kitchen with Nana and his parents, sobbing hysterically. It was the day his mother told him that Nana was leaving.

"Oh, stop whining," his mother had scolded in an icy voice. He had tried to run to Nana, but his mother had pulled him back by the shoulder with a firm grip.

"Act like a big boy," his father had admonished him. "You're too old for a baby-sitter anymore."

Devon had broken away from his mother and run to his nanny. She had tried to hide the tears in her eyes as she hugged him. "You be a big grown-up boy like your mama and daddy say," she had whispered.

This time his father had pulled him away. "Go to your room!" he had thundered.

Seven-year-old Devon had hidden just outside the door of the kitchen and overheard the brief, angry conversation between Nana and his parents. Nana had begged them to reconsider and let her stay on. He remembered his father telling her that he knew what was best for their son.

Devon swallowed hard. Then Nana had turned her back and walked away without ever really saying good-bye. He had never heard from her again. Through all the years of birthdays and Christmases, of other holidays and in between, there had never been a phone call—never a letter or even a card.

Devon turned the envelope over and over. Why had she contacted him now, after all these years? A voice in his head whispered the obvious answer—*money*.

He held the envelope between his palms for several minutes. He wanted to know what she had to say, but he was afraid too. He had been disappointed so many times that he was scared by the leap of hope his heart had taken when he saw her name.

Devon slid his fingers under a corner of the envelope flap and ripped along the crease. He pulled out a small white card with silver lettering.

"In sympathy," he read aloud. "OK," he whispered. "Let's see how sympathetic you really are."

He opened the card and began to read.

After a moment he bit his lip. Nana had run into a former employee of the Whitelaws who had told her about the death of his parents. She had tried to phone him again and again, but no one had answered. Devon's eyes blurred slightly as he read the last paragraph.

> I hope this card will find its way to you and that you will come to visit me here in Sweet Valley. You are always welcome in my home, Devon. I have missed you so terribly all these years. Please accept my invitation. It would mean so much to me.
>
> With love,
> Nana

Devon closed the card and put it beside him on the faded, stained blanket. He shut his eyes to hold back the tears.

"If you missed me so much, why didn't you let me know?" he whispered.

A long sigh escaped his lips. Would Nana lie to him and use him as his relatives had? He wanted—needed—to believe she really cared. Her card had sounded so sincere. . . .

The guy next door started blasting the country

music station again. Devon briefly considered banging on the wall once more. He raised his fist, then decided it wasn't worth the trouble.

He got to his feet and pulled his duffel bag out from under the bed. Then he began throwing his clothes into it. He was sick of feeling sorry for himself—sick of lying around acting defeated.

"Sweet Valley, California," he said, considering his next destination. For the first time in weeks he felt the corners of his mouth turn up into a smile. He pictured blue, cloudless skies and pristine beaches, an endless procession of beautiful California girls, all of them friendly and full of life.

Devon pushed the last of his clothes into the duffel bag and jerked the zipper closed. *I might as well go and find out whether Nana really cares or if she's just after my money,* he thought. Besides, what did he have to lose? He took a look around the room at the sagging mattress, worn carpet, and stained, peeling walls. He decided he didn't want to end up like the loser next door, holed up in his dingy pit of a room day after day. Whatever lay ahead in Sweet Valley had to be a whole lot better than this place.

Lila clutched her notebook against the front of her white dress as she threaded her way through the throngs of students in Sweet Valley High's crowded main hallway. All around her the tide of people hurried by, lockers slammed shut, and groups of kids chatted and laughed. Lila gritted her teeth.

Usually she felt like a part of all the cheerful chaos, but not today. Instead she was painfully aware of the whispers and stares and the way people seemed to stop in midsentence when she came near.

Lila squared her shoulders, lifted her head high, and forced herself to gaze back at her onlookers, nod, and say hello as she passed. But she felt like ducking into one of the empty rooms and curling up in a closet until the bell rang.

Lila caught a glimpse of some of the cheerleaders: Amy Sutton, Heather Mallone, Maria Santelli, and Annie Whitman, along with a few other friends, hanging out by the water fountain. *My real friends will stand by me,* she thought. She quickened her pace and hurried to meet them as if she were heading for an oasis in the desert.

"Hi, guys," she said cheerily when she reached the group. She waited for them to turn and welcome her, figuring they'd be full of questions about what had happened. Surely they wanted to hear all about how terribly the Sweet Valley Police Department had treated her.

Instead a hush fell over the small crowd.

"Uh . . . hi, Lila," Maria said, looking away quickly and running a hand over her curly brown hair.

"What's going on?" Annie asked in an obviously forced cheerful tone.

"That's a stupid question," Amy said, elbowing Annie in the ribs. Annie's cheeks flamed red, and she stared at her sneakers as if they were the most fascinating things on the planet.

"There's certainly a lot going on in the life of Sweet Valley's hottest criminal," Heather said with a sneer. She flipped her long blond hair over her shoulder and looked Lila up and down with disdain. "Tell me, Lila, are you planning to wear an innocent white dress to your trial, or will you go with something in, say, fire-engine red?"

Lila gasped as Amy stifled a snort of laughter. Lila and Heather had never been the best of friends, but Lila couldn't believe that Heather would want to hurt her this way. Could she possibly be more blatantly evil?

"Hey, Heather," Maria said, looking up. "Back off a little."

"Yeah," Annie chimed in, her voice quiet. "Innocent until proven guilty and all that."

"Whatever," Heather said with a shrug. "But I'd stay away from her if I were you guys. The Fowler heiress could turn out to be a hazard to your health."

With that, Heather turned and flounced away, Amy at her heels.

"Sorry, Li," Maria said with a tight smile. "I gotta get to class." Maria walked away, and Annie scurried after her, stopping long enough to send Lila a guilt-ridden glance over her shoulder.

Lila's mind spun out of control, and she felt sick to her stomach. *This isn't fair,* she wailed inwardly. *How could my friends be so cold?*

Taking a few deep breaths to prevent herself from crying, Lila leaned back against the cool wall. The most important thing was that she remain composed. She didn't want Heather to have the satisfaction of hearing about Lila's tearful breakdown in the hall.

Just when Lila thought she had control of herself, she saw something that made her stomach lurch all over again. Caroline Pearce, the most accomplished gossip at SVH, was barreling down the hall, heading straight for Lila. As she came closer, her grin stretched wider and wider. *Like a spider on the trail of a fly,* Lila thought.

She pushed herself away from the wall and tried to hurry past Caroline, but the tall redhead planted herself in Lila's path. Lila got a whiff of her pungent perfume and swallowed hard to keep from puking on Caroline's faux leather sandals.

"Lila!" Caroline cried. "I wondered when you'd be coming back to school." She dropped her voice to a confidential whisper. "Frankly, I admire your nerve." She blinked rapidly and shook her head. "If I knew everyone was calling me a criminal behind my back, well, I'd just *die*."

"Thanks for the vote of confidence, Caroline," Lila muttered. She tried to move on, but Caroline hurried along beside her.

"Even if everyone else thinks you bombed that restaurant, Lila, I'm not convinced," Caroline breathed. "I don't believe those rumors that you set fire to your house either." She flashed a self-satisfied look. Lila kept her eyes trained straight ahead and quickened her pace.

"You know, Lila, if you ever need a sympathetic ear, I'm here for you," Caroline said. She moved in closer and put her hand on Lila's arm. Her touch made Lila's skin crawl.

"You can tell me *anything*."

Lila felt an angry lump rising in her throat. *This is too much,* she thought. As if she would ever be stupid enough to trust Caroline of all people. Did the girl think that Lila was going to reveal exactly how she had constructed the bomb or something? She jerked back her arm.

"Crawl back under your rock, Caroline," she snapped. "Your act isn't fooling me." She pushed past the girl and continued down the hall, leaving Caroline staring after her, openmouthed.

The nerve of some people, Lila thought, straightening her skirt as she walked.

As she neared her locker Lila saw Jessica and Elizabeth approaching. She caught a breath in her throat. She had a fleeting moment of longing to pour out her heart to Jessica.

Lila swallowed hard. *I can't confide in her,* she reminded herself. Now that Lila's relationship with Steven had come between her and Jessica, she felt worlds apart from her ex–best friend. *Things will never be the same with us again,* she thought with a pang of regret.

If Jessica disapproved of my dating Steven before, it's probably worse now that I've been in jail, she realized. Lila looked the other way as Jessica and her sister came closer, intending to ignore them as she knew they would her.

"Hi, Lila," Jessica said warmly.

"How're you holding up?" Elizabeth asked in a soothing tone. Lila looked at them, confused and wary.

"OK, I guess," she said softly. She wanted to keep her guard up in case Jessica intended to scoff at her the way Heather had. "As well as can be expected."

Jessica bit her lip. "For what it's worth, I don't think you're guilty."

Lila gave Jessica a long look. She appeared

to be sincere, and Lila had known the girl long enough to be able to tell when she was lying. A wave of relief washed over her.

"Thanks, Jess," she murmured, her eyes filling with hot tears. She forced herself to keep her voice from quavering. Did this mean Jessica wanted to be friends again? Were Jessica and Elizabeth really going to stand by her? Lila turned toward her locker and spun the dial, not wanting them to see the tears of hope that had begun to spill over.

"Hang in there, Lila," Elizabeth said, patting her on the shoulder. "I'll see you later." Lila felt Elizabeth move away as she kept her blurry eyes fixed on her lock.

"Take care, Li," Jessica said, inching away.

"Bye," Lila said weakly. She looked up and watched Jessica walk off down the hall. Did Jessica really believe in her, or was she just being polite? Lila's heart ached for a time when she and Jessica would have been sauntering through school together, chatting about meaningless things like fashion and makeup. She sighed. Until just now she had almost forgotten how much she missed having Jessica as her best friend.

She remembered how great Jessica had been right after the fire. She had convinced Lila to go on a whirlwind shopping spree to replace all the clothes she had lost in the fire and to cheer Lila up.

At the time Lila had barely been able to get interested, but Jessica had persisted. In the end Lila had told Jessica to take the clothes home with her. With Fowler Crest in ruins she didn't have room for them anyway, and she just couldn't concentrate on the way she looked when her life was in such a shambles. But at least Jessica had started out with good intentions.

A pained grimace swept over Lila's face as she recalled how cold Jessica had turned when she'd found out that Lila was dating her brother. Lila's shoulders sagged under the heavy burden of the memory. She hated that they had let a guy come between them—even a guy as perfect as Steven. She and Jessica had been best friends all their lives. Was it really over for good?

Lila tossed her long brown hair behind her shoulders. That was the least of her worries, she realized. *I may miss Jessica, but I've got to make sure I stay out of jail.*

She was about to grab her French book when she spied an envelope propped up on the top shelf of her locker. She picked it up and turned it over curiously.

The stationery was nothing special. The envelope

looked like it came from one of those prepackaged sets at the drugstore. *Who would give me such a thing?* she wondered.

Lila tore open the envelope and pulled out a piece of ordinary computer paper. The minute she saw the signature, her heart leapt. It was a note from Steven. She pressed her lips together tightly. What would he say? He had given her the cold shoulder all the way home from the police station the other day, not understanding why she would rather spend some time at the spa than with him. After that, Lila hadn't heard from him. Until now. Her hands trembled as she started to read.

Moments later her lips curved into a gentle smile. She felt warm all over as his words leapt off the page and into her heart. Everything Heather and Amy and Caroline had said, the pained looks from Maria and Annie, slowly faded away.

Steven hoped she was all right. He missed her. He believed in her. She was his princess, and he loved and adored her.

Lila stopped reading for a moment and savored the romantic words. She suddenly longed to see him with a searing intensity.

Lila ran her fingers gently over the page as if she were caressing Steven's face. But as she read on, the smile disappeared from her lips. The sweet, romantic words had changed, and she didn't like what they said.

> I can just imagine our future. We'll have a simple wedding in my parents' backyard. There'll be family and a few friends—only the people we care about the most. And we can have a cookout and pool party after the ceremony.
> Then, after spending our honeymoon kayaking and camping in the mountains, we'll settle down in a modest house with a porch swing and a white picket fence. It will have a few extra bedrooms, of course, for all the little Wakefields we'll have running around. The girls will have your beauty, and the boys will have my intelligence.
> Life will be one big family barbecue. And with my beautiful wife by my side—with you by my side, Lila—I know I'll be successful in the D.A.'s office. The pay will be next to nothing, but it will be enough to support us, although we'll have to give up certain comforts. . . .

Lila could feel her blood boil with disappointment and anger. How could he think that she would be satisfied with staying home in some little shack, taking care of a bunch of brats? And just what "comforts" was he planning on giving up? Certainly not her trips to Aspen or her days at the spa or real necessities like manicures and champagne and escargot.

Who would she socialize with? A bunch of women who colored their hair with a kit at home and never set foot inside a salon? Who had no sense of fashion and wore sagging sweat-pants over their spreading backsides every day? Who clipped coupons and bought their furni-ture on sale from department stores? Lila felt faint.

She had thought her romance was so perfect. And then she had to read *this*.

Lila threw the letter back on the shelf and slammed her locker shut. *If that's what Steven has in mind for the future, he obviously has no idea who he's dealing with,* she fumed silently. She kicked the locker for emphasis, then winced when a bolt of pain shot from her toe all the way up her leg. Lila looked down at her injured foot. *Brilliant, Fowler,* she scolded herself. *Kick inanimate objects when you're wearing open-toed sandals.*

Straightening herself up, Lila tried to retain some semblance of calm. She tossed her hair over her shoulder and stalked down the hallway toward class, limping slightly but keeping her head high. *When I get through this day,* Lila promised herself, *I am going to give Steven Wakefield a piece of my mind.*

She swung open the door to her French classroom, and all eyes turned to stare at her. Lila's defiant spirit withered.

If I get through this day.

"I think Lila's just beginning to truly understand the complexities of Steven Wakefield," Elizabeth said with a giggle. The bell had just rung, signaling the start of first period, but Jessica had convinced Elizabeth to hang out long enough to see Lila's reaction. The two girls were huddled in the empty hallway around the corner from Lila's locker and had watched as she stormed off. Elizabeth brushed a strand of hair off her forehead and grinned at her sister.

"You mean the *simplicities* of Steven Wakefield," Jessica joked.

"You know, Jessica," Elizabeth began, starting to walk toward the stairwell, "when I first read that letter, I thought you were laying the whole Little House on the Prairie thing on a little too thick. But I've got to admit, I think it worked."

Jessica gave Elizabeth a satisfied smile as she strolled along at her side. "Everyone thinks you're the only writer in the family, but I've got talent too."

"As you never forget to remind anyone who will listen," Elizabeth quipped. She shifted her books to her other hip and sighed. Even though she was glad that their letter had had the desired effect, she couldn't help feeling a bit guilty about the way she and Jessica were treating Lila.

"Do you think we're doing the right thing?" Elizabeth asked as Jessica pushed through the doors to the stairwell. "Lila has been through a terrible time lately. Now we're lying to her."

Jessica's eyes widened, and she stopped in her tracks. "Elizabeth Wakefield, can you stop having a conscience for five seconds?" she shrieked.

"Keep your voice down," Elizabeth hissed as Jessica's shout echoed through the empty hallways. She halted on the second step and turned to look down at her sister. "All I'm saying is, we might have crossed a line by forging a letter from Steven."

"Maybe we did something sneaky," Jessica answered in a hoarse whisper. "But it's not like we really *lied*. That *is* the way Steven envisions his future."

"True," Elizabeth said thoughtfully. "And if it'll

keep Lila away from him, I guess it's worth it."

"Steven's happiness is the most important thing," Jessica said, stepping up and looking Elizabeth in the eyes. "We did this for him."

Elizabeth nodded. When Jessica put it that way, the letter didn't seem so bad. Once Steven realized how wrong he and Lila were for each other and they broke up, he'd probably even thank his sisters for doing him such a great favor. After all, he was usually just as logical and levelheaded as Elizabeth herself. He'd know that writing the letter was in his best interests.

Suddenly a lightbulb went off in Elizabeth's mind.

"You know, Jess," she said, draping her arm around her sister's shoulders and starting up the stairs again, "our next project is to get him back together with Billie."

"Whoa! I've created a monster!" Jessica said, pulling away and skipping up the last few steps. "One plan at a time, Liz!"

"OK! OK!" Elizabeth laughed as she breezed past Jessica into the hallway of the second floor. "Operation Breakup is fully under way!"

Chapter 4

Steven paused and took a deep breath before entering the D.A.'s office. He wondered if he should have bothered wearing his gray wool suit. Why dress for work when you probably wouldn't be working?

He realized he was grinding his teeth and stopped. Wearing a suit was a show of respect, he decided. He was going to show how he felt about the internship and the legal profession even if he was going to be fired.

Steven started to open the door, noticed his hand was shaking, and pulled back. He had to try to look professional. Wiping his hand on his thigh, he squared his shoulders. Then he grasped the brass handle, swung open the door, and entered the office with what he hoped was a confident-looking stride. But when he thought about seeing the D.A., he felt about as confident as a turkey on Thanksgiving.

The moment Steven entered the office, he could feel everyone's eyes on him. But they all looked away before he met their gaze. *That can't be a good sign,* Steven thought. The knot in his stomach tightened. His coworkers seemed to be expecting the worst, as did he.

As Steven walked toward his cubicle he could hear his heart pounding in his ears. Suddenly the D.A. stuck his head out of his office as if he had picked Steven up on his internal radar.

"Wakefield, I want you in here right now," Garrison barked.

Steven lifted his chin. *I had to do what I believed was right,* he reminded himself. *And I didn't think it was right to leave Lila in that jail cell. If that's going to cost me my job, so be it.* Steven took a deep breath and headed into Joe Garrison's office.

The D.A. paced behind his huge black desk, his meaty hands clasped behind his back. "Sit down, Steven," he said quietly. "What I have to say won't take long."

Steven slid into a leather chair and pretended to flick a speck of lint from his lapel in an attempt at nonchalance. His hands were still shaking slightly. He rested them on his knees and forced himself to look the D.A. in the eye.

Garrison returned Steven's gaze and cleared his throat before he spoke. "I expected great things from you this summer, Wakefield. You came very highly recommended, and your grades were excellent. You carried yourself well too, with maturity and confidence. I thought you had terrific potential, but . . ."

Steven's heart did a double back flip and then sank down to the soles of his shoes when he heard the word *but*. He found himself squirming in his chair and forced himself to be still. Somehow he managed to keep his gaze steady.

"But things didn't work out the way I'd hoped," the D.A. went on. "Being able to separate professional and private life is extremely important in this profession."

"Sir," Steven began tentatively, "my belief in Lila's innocence has nothing to do with our personal relationship."

"That's bull and you know it, Steven!" Garrison thundered. Steven's mouth snapped shut as the D.A.'s face darkened from pink to crimson. His eyes flashed dangerously, and Steven pressed himself back into his seat. Garrison sat down behind his desk and took a deep breath, obviously trying to compose himself.

"An attorney has to think with his head, not his heart," Garrison said quietly, staring at Steven with a grave expression. "In the case of Lila Fowler, you showed me you're not able to do that. On top of that, you flagrantly disobeyed my instructions not to become involved with the girl."

The D.A. unclasped his hands and laid them flat on the desk. "This internship is over," Garrison said firmly.

The air whooshed from Steven's lungs as he saw all his dreams of a career in law burst into flames before his eyes. He opened his mouth to protest, but all that came out was a pathetic gasp.

"My report to the school will be as fair as I can make it," Garrison continued, "but I'll have to tell the truth. I only hope that you've learned something from this experience and that you are able to put it to good use." The D.A. stood, walked to the door, and placed his hand on the knob. "Clean out your desk before you leave."

"Can I say something, sir?" Steven asked as he rose to his feet. He wasn't ready to retreat with his tail between his legs. He looked down at the D.A. and was suddenly grateful that he had height advantage.

The D.A. stuck his hands in his pockets. "Make it brief," he said crisply.

"All right," Steven began. "You said an attorney has to be objective—to think with his head and not with his heart. When I bailed Lila Fowler out of jail, I wasn't thinking with my heart. I was thinking logically. And logic tells me that every shred of evidence you have against Lila is circumstantial."

Garrison rolled his eyes and walked back to his desk. "You're just a rookie, Wakefield. You can't see what's staring you right in the face."

Steven crossed the room in one long stride and leaned over the large desk to look Garrison straight in the eyes.

"What's staring me right in the face," Steven said defiantly, "is a law enforcer who's victimizing an innocent sixteen-year-old girl because finding the real culprit is just too complex."

The D.A. jumped to his feet, his fists clenched and his jaw set. Suddenly Steven's height advantage was inconsequential. Staring at the powerful, enraged man, Steven realized he could be in for the fight of his life if Garrison decided to take a swing.

"How dare you?" the D.A. roared, beads of perspiration popping up along his forehead. "Get out of this office right now before I make you wish you never met me."

Too late, Steven thought as he straightened up. He kept his eyes fixed on Garrison's face for a prolonged moment and then turned and walked slowly toward the door. His knees were like Jell-O, but there was no way he was going to let Garrison see how scared he really was.

As he walked to his cubicle no one in the office said a word. Steven was sure they had all heard the end of his exchange with the D.A. They probably all thought they would be fired if they were caught speaking to him.

Steven told himself not to look back. His internship might be over, but he had to focus on the task at hand—proving Lila's innocence. He couldn't waste any time feeling sorry for himself.

Steven stiffly went through the motions of cleaning out his desk. He quickly opened drawers and started pulling out items that belonged to him—the silver pen his parents had given him, his leather appointment book, some notebooks he'd brought in. He stuffed everything into his briefcase at random.

Suddenly something fell out of one of the notebooks and fluttered to the linoleum floor. Steven bent down to pick it up and drew his breath in sharply. It was a picture of Billie from a hike they'd taken together only a couple of months ago. She smiled out at him from the glossy surface, her blue eyes twinkling and her chestnut hair pulled back in a ponytail.

A pang of regret stabbed Steven's heart as he sank into the rickety wooden chair at his desk. The encounter with Garrison slipped from his mind as he stared into Billie's laughing eyes. Lila had been so constant in his thoughts that he hadn't even thought of Billie in days. Now he was surprised at how much he missed her.

Everything was so comfortable with Billie, he thought.

Steven recalled the picnics, the trips to the lake, all the nights they had curled up together with a pizza and a good video. *Things that Lila would never enjoy doing.*

Feelings of confusion tore through him. He had thought he was over Billie, but he couldn't be if he was suddenly so overcome with emotion.

He held her picture tightly. *It's funny in a sad, strange way that it was this internship that broke us up,* Steven mused. Billie had thought Steven was putting his work ahead of her. But now he had lost both the internship and the love of his life. He shook his head as he replaced the picture in his notebook.

Billie had been so cold to him in the last days before he left. *Maybe I didn't try hard enough to make her understand,* Steven thought. *Maybe*

I just couldn't find the right words to explain that my work didn't come before *Billie—it was just important in a different way.* He sighed. It wouldn't do any good to think about that now. It was time to get on with his life, and that meant getting out of this office.

Suddenly a thought popped into his head. The evidence room. Once he left the building, there was no way he'd ever get a chance to look at the Fowler case evidence again. If he was still going to help Lila clear her name, he was going to have to get one last look at the items locked away in that room.

Quickly he glanced around the office. Now the fact that no one wanted to make eye contact with him seemed like a blessing. It would make sneaking into the restricted area unnoticed a whole lot easier. Steven cast a nervous glance at the door to Garrison's office. It was closed. It was now or never.

Steven casually wandered down the hall and into the law library, doing his best to blend in with the bustling office activity. The shelves in the large room were lined with thick volumes bound in dark green and brown. Steven had spent several hours there doing research for the D.A., sometimes working far into the night.

Steven walked swiftly through the empty library

to the small, dingy room at the far end where evidence was kept. A guard stood outside with a sign-in sheet. Steven swallowed nervously as he approached. If the guard knew that Steven had been fired, there was no chance he would get into the room.

But the tall, blond officer merely handed Steven the clipboard and pen. Steven scribbled his name and the date. If anyone questioned him later, he could tell them he was in there before he got fired.

Steven handed the clipboard back to the guard and slipped into the room, closing the door softly behind him.

The cubbyholes lining the walls held all kinds of items—gloves and sunglasses, bags containing fragments of hair and scraps of clothing, spoons and broken shards of mirror. Each piece of evidence was tagged and numbered for future reference in a trial or hearing.

Steven walked up to the section marked Fowler Crest Case. *It's still my case, whether I'm working for the D.A. or not,* he assured himself fiercely.

He examined the items he'd already studied dozens of times—the matches found in Lila's pocket, the monogrammed gloves that still smelled of gasoline, the bomb paraphernalia.

Then something he hadn't seen before caught his eye. He glanced over his shoulder nervously before picking it up.

It appeared to be a piece of the bomb that had caused the chaos at Palomar House. What could this charred, melted hunk of metal prove?

Steven turned the item over, and his heart pounded. Painted on the surface was a soda brand logo—a logo that was very familiar. "ProSport Lemon," Steven whispered.

A picture of John Pfeifer's untidy desk at the *Oracle* office flashed through his mind—the piles of papers, the candy wrappers, and the half-empty soda can. *ProSport Lemon soda.*

Suddenly Steven felt charged with electricity. He wanted to run into the D.A.'s office holding the fragment of the soda can and tell him how it unquestionably linked John Pfeifer to the restaurant bombing—and to framing Lila for the crime. Which obviously meant that he also framed her for the torching of Fowler Crest. He was halfway to the door before he stopped short.

Don't make the same mistake you did before, he told himself. *You went to the D.A. too soon, without thinking everything out.*

Steven returned the tagged fragment of metal to the cubbyhole. He knew that if he removed it from the evidence room, it would automatically be considered tampered with, and it would be inadmissible in court. He couldn't risk that. It was the one piece of evidence that could clear Lila's name.

Steven crossed to the door slowly this time. He had some work to do. And until he was certain of every last fact, he wasn't even going to *try* to talk to the D.A.

I did learn something during this internship, Garrison, Steven thought with a wry smile. *If you want something done right, you better do it yourself.*

Lila studied Steven's hands as he clutched the steering wheel of his yellow VW. Such strong hands, yet they could be gentle too. She remembered those hands stroking her hair as he held her, as he kissed her. . . .

A flash of irritation banished the image from her mind. Steven had told her there was an important development in the case. But they had been driving for nearly fifteen minutes, and he hadn't even hinted at what the news might be.

Lila fidgeted in her seat. Her emotions were jumbled and confused. In spite of the supercharged electricity between them, maybe she and Steven weren't meant to be. She felt a prickle of disappointment as she remembered his letter.

Lila glanced at Steven's profile. *I can't tell him how I feel about that letter now,* she told herself. *Not when he lost his job because of me.*

"You said you had something to tell me, Steven." Lila tried to keep the edge of impatience out of her voice. "What is it?" She smoothed her black-and-white-checked skirt.

"You're just going to have to wait a little while longer," Steven said, keeping his eyes on the road.

"Why?" Lila blurted. "What kind of game are you playing? You said you had to see me right away so I canceled my manicure, which, by the way, I needed desperately. So why don't you just tell me already?"

Steven just laughed and shook his head.

"I'm not going to *tell* you, I'm going to *show* you," he said.

Lila watched, confused, as Steven turned the car into the parking lot of the Shop & Hop convenience store.

"Just be patient and you'll see," he said.

Patience wasn't Lila's strong suit. "See *what?*" she snapped.

"Take it easy," he said with a lighthearted chuckle. "When you see what I have to show you, I have a hunch you'll be very happy."

71

Steven was smiling as he pulled into a parking space right in front of the tall windows that made up the front wall of the little store.

His joviality grated on Lila's already fraying nerves. *Calm down,* she told herself. *If he's really cracked the case, this whole nightmare could be over before brunch tomorrow.*

Steven hopped out of the car and crossed to open Lila's door.

"Come on, let's go get a soda," he said, offering his hand. Lila took it but continued to pout as they made their way inside.

"Steven," she said as she eyed the garish posters advertising one-dollar gallons of milk and various brands of ice cream. "If you wanted to get something to drink, we could've gone downtown for an espresso. Or at least to the Dairi Burger . . ."

"We had to come here," Steven interrupted.

What was he talking about? What was so special about this cheesy convenience store? Steven opened one of the beverage cases. A blast of cold air hit Lila in the face. She backed away. "I'm not thirsty."

"Go ahead, grab a soda," Steven urged.

Did I never notice how weird he is, or is this the first time he's ever acted this strange? Lila wondered. She reminded herself that he had

72

just lost his job. Maybe that explained his odd behavior. She let out a sigh and grabbed a bottle of sparkling seltzer.

Steven snatched it from her hand. Lila almost yelped in surprise.

"Steven, I'm beginning to think you've lost it," she said.

"I promise I'm not crazy," he answered, returning the seltzer to the case. "I just thought you might like to try something different for a change. Be adventurous." He took another can of soda and gave it to her. "How about this one?"

"ProSport soda?" Lila asked, holding up the can. The label was black with huge red letters and a basketball drawn to look like it was bouncing out at her. Now she was sure Steven had gone off the deep end. Just to humor him, she ran her finger across the list of ingredients.

"Are they serious?" Lila blurted. "I can't believe what they put in this stuff—loads of potassium and vitamins, and *calories*. You must be kidding, Steven. I would never drink this in a million years."

Lila saw a smile flicker across Steven's face. This was exasperating! The more annoyed Lila became, the happier Steven seemed.

"Is something funny?" she snapped.

"No." Steven shook his head, but his smile

widened. "I just think you're proving my theory."

Lila tapped her foot impatiently. "I wish you'd tell me what's going on," she said. She started to shove the soda back into the refrigerator, but Steven pulled her hand back gently.

"Don't worry about the calories," he said.

Lila stared at him. He had said they were going to talk about her case, and all he had done was taken her to this dive on the highway. Now he was forcing some icky sports drink on her. "Please tell me this somehow has something to do with the case," Lila said, defeated. "Did the arsonist douse the mansion with this stuff before he lit the fire or something? I bet this junk could be substituted for gasoline."

Steven laughed wholeheartedly this time.

"Trust me, you'll understand in just a minute," he said as he walked to the counter to pay for the soda.

"You've got five more minutes, Steven," Lila called to him as she breezed by the counter and out the door. "After that, I'm calling the loony bin."

Chapter 5

Steven walked out of the convenience store, grabbed Lila's hand, and led her to the grassy area next to the asphalt. It was time to prove his theory once and for all.

"Take this," Steven said, holding the can of ProSport soda out to her. He noticed her delicate hands were trembling.

"Honestly, this is so weird," Lila muttered. As she started to crack the tab on the can Steven put his hand over hers.

"Wait! Don't open it," he said.

Steven watched Lila's mouth twist into a pout. She let her breath out in an explosive little burst. "Honestly, Steven," she said. "You're being really strange. First you insist on buying me a soda I don't even like. Then when I'm actually going to drink it, you stop me." She tossed her hair impatiently.

"Calm down, Lila," Steven said with a grin. "Where's your sense of adventure?"

"My idea of an adventure is a cruise to the Caribbean," Lila said, rolling her eyes. "*Not* a rendezvous at the local Stop & Hop."

The grin disappeared from Steven's face. *When did she get so whiny?* he thought. *She's acting like a cranky child.* Then he remembered that she must be under a lot of stress. It was unfair to keep her in the dark about his theory any longer. But he didn't want to tell her until he was absolutely convinced he was right.

"Listen, Lila," Steven began, placing his hands on her shoulders and looking her directly in the eyes, "I don't want you to *drink* the soda, I want you to *throw* it."

"What?" Lila screeched.

Steven turned her gently toward the grassy field and pointed to a line of trees about fifty yards away.

"I want you to throw the can of soda up and out, as high as you can and as far as you can at the same time," he directed.

As Lila opened her mouth to speak Steven gently touched a finger to her lips. "Shhh, Lila, please. Just do it."

Lila took a deep breath, rolled her eyes again,

76

and tossed the soda can into the air. It made a small arc and landed a few yards away.

Steven trotted over and retrieved it. "Try harder," he said. "Give it all you've got."

"I'm not exactly football player material," Lila said huffily. She drew back her arm and threw the soda can into the air. This time it made a higher arc and landed farther away. "That's the best I can do," she said breathlessly.

"Great!" Steven said brightly. It was more than great—it was perfect! He retrieved the soda can once more. "Watch this." He snapped back his arm and grunted as he threw the can high into the air. Then he turned back to Lila and grinned.

"Bravo," Lila said sarcastically. "*Now* are you going to tell me what's going on?" she asked, putting her hands on her hips.

Steven took both her hands in his and clasped them tightly. He was so excited about breaking the case and proving Lila innocent, he could barely contain himself.

"I saw the bomb come through the restaurant window," Steven explained. "It broke the glass near the top, and those windows are at least ten feet high."

Lila still looked confused.

"Don't you see?" Steven ran his hand over Lila's hair. "I had to throw the can as hard as I could to get it that high. You couldn't possibly have thrown it that hard. Besides, it would never even have occurred to you to purchase ProSport."

"But I still don't understand what ProSport has to do with anything," Lila said, knitting her brows.

"Today, before I left the office, I found a fragment of a ProSport can among the bomb paraphernalia in the evidence room," Steven said. "It was all twisted and a little charred, but I could make out the label as clear as day."

"That's great, Steven," Lila said halfheartedly. "But how is that going to prove I'm innocent? Just because I wouldn't buy ProSport for myself doesn't mean I wouldn't buy it to make a bomb. Any lawyer could argue that."

"You're right," Steven said. "But I wasn't counting on the can proving you innocent. I think the fact that you can't throw to save your life does that. I was really counting on the ProSport proving someone *else* guilty."

"What do you mean?" Lila asked, crossing her arms over her chest and narrowing her eyes.

"The day Liz and I checked out John Pfeifer's desk at the *Oracle*, guess what I found?" Steven asked excitedly.

Lila looked a bit ill at the mention of John

Pfeifer's name. The color drained from her face, and for a moment Steven was afraid she might faint. He reached out and took her hand, squeezing it to reassure her.

"John's desk?" she breathed.

"I found a can of ProSport soda," he said in a soothing tone. "It was even the same flavor as the can used in the bombing."

"Are you sure?" Lila asked quietly, her eyes dazed.

"Totally sure," Steven answered. He led her back to his car, opened the door, and helped her into the seat. She looked so fragile all of a sudden—the way she always looked when the subject of John Pfeifer was raised. Steven knelt on the blacktop in front of Lila, whose feet were dangling from the open door.

"I'd like to kill him for everything he's put you through," Steven said, reaching up and caressing Lila's milky white cheek.

"Do you really think he's behind all this?" Lila asked quietly. "I mean, do you think this new evidence really proves he's guilty?"

Steven looked up into Lila's brown eyes and noticed they were swimming in tears.

"It's a jock soda for a jock who would have been strong enough to toss that bomb through the restaurant window," Steven said firmly. "Plus he has a motive for trying to ruin your life because he thinks you ruined his. I really believe we have our man. I just want to make sure I have enough for an airtight case before I go to the D.A."

Lila took a deep breath and let it out shakily. She didn't look too happy about the news.

"Lila, I know this whole thing has been tough on you," Steven said carefully. "Aren't you happy that it's almost over?"

Lila blinked a few times and then looked into his eyes. "I just wonder if we'll still be together when this is all over," she said in a voice barely above a whisper.

There was a sharp pang in Steven's heart, and he sucked in a quick breath. He was surprised that Lila's words made him so uncomfortable. An image of Billie appeared in his mind. He pushed it away and tried to focus on the girl who was here with him.

"Sure, we'll be together," he said slowly. He watched a corner of Lila's mouth curl downward.

She folded her arms. "Not if you want us to be together in a house full of dogs and babies, having barbecues in the backyard," she said.

Steven's eyes widened. "Where did *that* come from?"

Lila's eyebrows shot up. "Well, isn't that your dream of the future? A little house with a white picket fence and dogs and babies crawling all over the place? One of those tacky plastic kids' wading pools in the backyard?"

Steven continued to stare at Lila as he tilted his head to one side. "Yeah, sort of," he said. "Although not necessarily the tacky kiddie pool. Is there something wrong with that?"

Lila gave a short, harsh laugh. "Well, yeah, I think there's something wrong with that. It's not exactly what I pictured for myself. I want a much more sophisticated kind of life."

Steven was totally shocked by Lila's sudden shift from quivering victim to angry snob. And who said he was going to ask her to marry him anyway? He was only eighteen, for Pete's sake!

"Caviar and champagne, that's what's important to you, right?" Steven said. He couldn't keep the trace of a sneer out of his voice.

Now it was Lila's turn to be indignant. "What's wrong with caviar and champagne? What's wrong with wanting to go to glamorous places and do exciting things?"

Steven stood up and looked down at Lila. "Let's just chill out," he said. "Why are we fighting about this anyway? We've got something more important to do. I want to prove your innocence and clear your name. Let's forget about life choices for now and focus on the task at hand."

Lila swallowed and looked up into Steven's

eyes. "You're right," she whispered. "I'm so glad you believe I'm not guilty. I was beginning to think *everyone* had turned against me."

"Not a chance," Steven said as Lila pulled her legs inside the car and closed the door. Steven walked around the front of the VW and hopped in behind the steering wheel.

He reached over and touched a finger to Lila's chin, turning her to face him. He stared at her intently.

"I've never doubted your innocence for a moment," he lied. There was a time when the D.A.'s doubts had filtered in, but that was all in the past. There was no reason to tell Lila about it now.

Lila smiled at him warmly—the first kind look she'd given him all day.

"Let's go wrap this thing up," Steven said, turning the key in the ignition.

"Where are we going?" Lila asked.

"To the *Oracle* office," Steven answered as he pulled out of his parking spot. "The more evidence we have, the better. And from what I've seen of John Pfeifer, I don't think he's levelheaded enough to have covered all his tracks."

A warm breeze blew against Devon's face as he rode his motorcycle through Sweet Valley.

The town was even more beautiful than he had imagined. He traveled along pristine streets lined with trees and flowers, and all the people seemed to be smiling as if they hadn't a care in the world. Everywhere he looked, there was another beautiful girl.

Devon drove past a slim blonde wearing impossibly short shorts. She flashed him a smile, and Devon grinned back. He almost laughed at himself for feeling so giddy, but he couldn't help it. Even though he wasn't sure about Nana's motivations, there was something about this place that told him he had finally come home. But Devon wasn't sold on living in Sweet Valley—not by a long shot. Nana would be the deciding factor.

Devon felt a rush of anticipation surge through his veins. So many years had passed since he had seen Nana. *Can I trust her?* Devon wondered. He gripped the handlebars tightly and steered his motorcycle around a hairpin turn. The old question returned. *Can I ever trust anyone again?*

As Devon turned onto Hummingbird Lane his head was clear and his thoughts were cool and rational. *Don't expect anything,* he told himself. *That way you won't be disappointed.*

Devon glimpsed the number thirteen on a wooden mailbox and turned into the driveway beside Nana's small, neat house. He felt butter-flies stir in his stomach as he took in the tiny lawn, white shutters, and window boxes filled with red flowers. He heaved himself off his seat and steadied himself, wondering if the weakness in his knees was the result of hours on the road or nervousness.

How will Nana look? he wondered. Would their old bond reappear, or would they feel strained and awkward? Would this be the place he finally found an honest heart, or was she an-other phony who would try to trick him out of his money? Devon realized his palms were sweaty, and he wiped them on the front of his jeans. *I might as well get this over with,* he thought.

Slowly Devon made his way up the cobblestone walk and rapped on the front door. His heart beat faster as he heard the faint sound of footsteps ap-proaching from inside. The curtain that hung in the small glass pane in the center of the door was pushed aside, and Devon held his breath. He caught a glimpse of two very familiar eyes just be-fore the door swung open.

"Devon!" the woman cried, the corners of her blue eyes crinkling as she smiled. "You're really here."

She reached up to hug him tightly and then pulled back as if to get a better look at him.

Devon felt a sudden, overwhelming wave of emotion. He had thought he would never see Nana again, and now here she was, standing less than two feet away.

Devon looked at Nana in silence for a moment. In spite of the years that had passed, she looked almost exactly the same as he remembered. Her hair was gray instead of auburn, but she still wore it pinned on top of her head. Her blue eyes twinkled youthfully although there were faint lines around them.

What shocked Devon most was how little she was. He had somehow expected he'd still look up at her the way he had when he was a boy. Instead he found that he towered over her.

"You've grown so tall," Nana said, as if reading his mind. A look of pride came over her face. She took his hand and led him into the house.

"You've got a cozy place here," Devon said as he put down his duffel bag. Everywhere he looked, he saw Nana's personal touches—the doilies she had crocheted, the pictures of plants and flowers on the walls, the china vase full of daffodils.

"Thank you, dear," Nana replied. She laughed lightly. "I moved into this little house ten years ago, when I left Connecticut." There was a little catch in her voice as she said those last words.

Nana paused a beat and then continued on

85

cheerily. "I was sure I'd be able to get something bigger soon, but it just didn't work out
that way."

Devon felt a prickle of suspicion. *Maybe you
think you can buy a better place now with my
money,* he thought. But he couldn't help feeling a
moment of hope that it wasn't the case.

Devon's roaming eyes settled on a framed picture on the mantelpiece. He felt an inexplicable
spark of recognition. Curious, he crossed the room
and picked up the frame to examine the photo. It
depicted a boy standing beside a rocking horse.
Devon remembered the toy an instant before he
recognized his own face.

"It's *me*," he said incredulously.

Nana's mouth curved into a gentle smile. "I've
kept it here for years," she said. "And I've looked
at it every day."

Devon swallowed. For a moment he felt emotion pulling at his heartstrings. But in the next instant he heard a warning bell sound in his head.

*Did she really keep that photo on the mantel
all these years?* he asked himself. He wanted to
believe it was true. On the other hand, she could
have unpacked it and put it there to make him
think she cared. He hated himself for being so
suspicious. *But after the way I've been treated, I
can't help it,* he thought.

86

He was so deep in thought, Nana's voice startled him.

"Before we catch up," Nana said, "I want to show you something. Follow me." She led the way to the back of the house.

"I won't hear of you staying in a hotel," Nana said as she walked down a narrow hallway. "I fixed up the spare room for you."

Devon followed her into a small room with wood-paneled walls. White curtains hung in a large window that took up most of the back wall and bathed the room in sunlight. There was a small dresser and desk, and a patchwork quilt was spread over the surface of a neatly made bed.

"I stitched it myself," she said. "Does it look familiar?"

Devon felt as if his heart had rolled over in his chest. Suddenly he remembered. He had played with his toys at Nana's feet as she sewed the squares together.

Just before Nana had pointed out the quilt, he had been about to protest—to tell her that he couldn't stay with her because he didn't want to inconvenience her. He had hoped staying in a hotel would help him maintain his distance and keep a hold on his emotions.

Devon exhaled a long sigh as he ran his fingers through his long brown bangs. *I was sure I learned my lesson about being taken in by people,* he said to himself. *Now I'm standing here with my eyes practically tearing up.* He squared his shoulders and told himself to get a grip. But as he looked into Nana's gentle, smiling face he knew it wasn't going to be easy.

Elizabeth spied her sister walking by in the hallway outside the *Oracle* office. She jumped up from her chair so fast that she nearly tore the hem of her plaid skirt when it caught on a corner of the seat. She yanked the fabric free and ran to the doorway.

"Jessica!" she called. "Come here, I've got to tell you something."

Jessica turned, and curiosity flickered in her blue-green eyes. She headed back toward the office, the pleats of her red miniskirt swinging around her legs as she walked.

Elizabeth pulled her inside and shut the door. The two girls were alone in the office.

"You'll never guess who was just here," she said breathlessly.

Jessica rolled her eyes. "I don't have time for guessing games, Liz. Why don't you just tell me?"

Elizabeth shook her pale blond hair off her shoulders. "Honestly, Jessica, I was only using a figure of speech. I didn't really mean for you to

88

guess. Lila and Steven were just here."

Jessica's face twisted into a sour expression. "Together?" she squealed.

Elizabeth nodded rapidly. "They were together, all right. They were looking for evidence to tie John Pfeifer to the restaurant bombing—and to burning down Fowler Crest," she explained.

Jessica sighed and sank into a chair. "Bummer," she said. "I was hoping that letter would do the trick. Maybe I should have written that Steven would expect his wife to wear polyester pants and housecoats. Now *that* would have sent Lila running for the hills."

"Probably," Elizabeth said, cracking a reluctant smile. "But the point is, it didn't work."

Elizabeth sat down facing Jessica and fiddled with a pencil on her desk. "I have to tell you, Jess, the thought of those two together *worries* me."

"It worries me too," Jessica said, a disgusted look on her face. "What if he invites her over for dinner and we have to watch them making eyes at each other? I don't think I could . . ."

"Jess, that's not what I meant!" Elizabeth exclaimed, although the idea of Steven mooning over Lila did make her want to vomit. "Lila's under investigation. Now Steven is out of a job, and she's the reason." Elizabeth tapped her foot on the floor. "I can't believe getting fired didn't shock him into giving up the case. What if Lila *is* guilty? He's playing right into her hands by going after John."

Jessica rolled her eyes. "Not this again!"

"It *is* a possibility," Elizabeth said, leaning forward. "After all, the D.A. thinks she's the prime suspect. Steven's association with her might have ruined his whole career."

Jessica leaned back in her chair, folded her arms, and frowned. "Well, *Steven* doesn't believe she's guilty, and I think he's pretty smart. I don't think he'd let his emotions interfere with his legal thinking either." Her frown deepened. "I *do* believe his thinking is clouded when it comes to love, though. Even a moron could tell that those two are total opposites." She chewed her bottom lip.

Elizabeth stood up. "Well, even if we have a difference of opinion about *why* Steven and Lila shouldn't be together, we still agree that they *shouldn't*." She walked over to her computer and sat down. "I saved the letter you typed from Steven to Lila. I'm going to take a look at it and try my luck at a letter of my own."

Jessica sat bolt upright, and Elizabeth couldn't resist a smile.

"*You're* going to fake a letter?" Jessica asked. Her eyes widened with amazement. "Why, Elizabeth

Wakefield, I didn't think you had it in you."

Elizabeth's smile widened. "I know. You thought being underhanded and sneaky was your department," she said as her fingers began clicking across the keyboard. "But if you can write, I can be devious."

She felt a little tingle of satisfaction at being able to shock her sister. *I'm not the straitlaced little goody-goody you think I am,* she said to herself.

Chapter 6

"Thanks, Nana—this is great," Devon said as he watched her pile a second helping of fried chicken, corn on the cob, and mashed potatoes onto his plate. He had forgotten that this was his favorite childhood meal and was touched that Nana had remembered and gone to the trouble of preparing it.

"I'm glad you like it, dear," Nana replied. "When you were a little boy, you used to get the biggest smile on your face when I fixed it for you."

As Devon felt more memories come rushing back he realized he was beginning to get used to these waves of nostalgia. Being around Nana seemed to spark memories he had long since buried deep in the recesses of his mind.

Devon had rarely eaten dinner with his

mother and father. He wasn't permitted to disturb his parents while they took their meals at the long mahogany table in the dining room. He had almost always eaten his dinner with Nana in the kitchen. While they ate, Nana would ask him questions and talk to him as seriously as if he'd been another adult. She was the only one who had ever even treated him like a human being.

Take it easy, Devon told himself as he slathered butter on the corn with his fork. There were lots of questions he wanted answered before he let himself trust Nana. He'd been burned twice before and was determined to be cautious—even though maintaining his cool hadn't been easy so far when it came to Nana.

Devon put down his fork. "I really don't think I should stay here," he said. When Nana started to interrupt, he motioned for silence. "You're busy running that preschool all day, and this house is nice, but it's small. I don't want to be a burden."

Nana patted Devon's hand quickly. "Nonsense," she said with a reassuring smile. "I already told you I'd love having you here. You can come and go as you please, and we can enjoy each other's company. All these years I've been hoping to one day see you again." Devon heard a little catch in her voice.

For an instant his heart thawed. Then an icy shot of anger surged through his veins. He had believed in his relatives and then been devastated when their kindness turned out to be an act. The words tumbled out of his mouth before he had a chance to think.

"If you dreamed of seeing me all these years, why didn't you ever try to visit me?" he asked. Suddenly he recalled how he had asked himself the same question over and over as a boy and always felt heartbroken when he couldn't think of an answer. The memory fueled his anger. He fought to keep his voice calm and even.

"Why didn't you phone me? Why didn't you write? I never got a single letter. You never even sent me a card on my birthday or at Christmas." He threw down his napkin. When he looked up, he saw that Nana's face was pale and there was a pinched look around her mouth. She held one hand curled up near her throat.

"Devon, you must believe me . . . I—I wanted to contact you," she said. "But this was . . . well, the first time I was able."

Devon stirred in his chair. He let out a snort of impatience. "And you expect me to believe that?" he demanded. "It's been years!" The words hung in the air between them.

"Please don't ask me any questions," Nana

said shakily. "I can't tell you why I couldn't reach you before now. You have to believe me. Trust me."

Devon's eyes searched her face. He took a deep breath in an attempt to calm himself. "You were able to get in touch with me this time. How come?" His eyes narrowed. "What made you try harder?"

"I—I just did," Nana stammered. She reached across the table and put a hand on Devon's arm. "Things just made it . . . *difficult* in the past."

Devon drummed his fingers on the table. "What was different this time?" He regarded her coolly. "This former employee of ours you ran into—did he say something that suddenly made you want to have me around?"

Nana blinked rapidly. "I don't know what you mean."

Devon studied Nana's face, waiting for a crack in her innocent expression. There was none. But maybe that just meant she was a good actress.

"Do you really want me to stay here?" he asked bluntly.

"Of course I do," Nana said earnestly. "You were like a son to me, Devon."

Devon felt his throat close up when he heard Nana call him *son*. It sounded so different when she said it than it had when his parents had said it. His chest felt tight. Coming from Nana, the word sounded as if it actually meant something.

You've been taken in by people who seemed to care before, Devon reminded himself. But he could feel himself aching to believe Nana while at the same time part of him fought against it.

Devon slid back his chair. "All right," he said. "I'll stay for a while. But I can't pay you anything. Some people thought I inherited a lot of money, but I didn't. My parents left me broke." He watched Nana's expression carefully. A look of horror came over her face.

"Oh, that's *terrible*," she said. "But it doesn't make any difference to me. I wouldn't dream of taking your money."

Devon looked down at his plate. *We'll see,* he said to himself. *We'll see.*

Elizabeth pushed open the door to the Wakefield house and tossed her keys into her purse. Jessica was right on her heels.

"I've got so much to do before Todd comes over," Elizabeth said. "I've got to study for chemistry, finish an article for the *Oracle,* and get started on my poetry project." She placed her purse on the table by the door.

"You'll manage," Jessica said as she waltzed into

the front hall behind Elizabeth. "You always do. Come on, let's go into the den for a few minutes and watch *Teen Talk*."

Elizabeth's determination to get her work done wavered. *Teen Talk* was an afternoon show that featured interviews with current teen celebrities as well as a fashion section and other topics of interest. It would be nice to relax for a couple of minutes before she hit the books.

"OK," she said as she followed her sister to the den. "But just for a little while."

Jessica swung open the den door and stopped in her tracks. Elizabeth narrowly avoided slamming into her and looked over Jessica's shoulder to see what had startled her sister. Steven was slumped on the sofa, staring straight ahead with a bewildered expression on his face. There was a letter in his hand.

Elizabeth shot Jessica a surprised glance. "I didn't think Steven would get his mail so fast," she whispered. "It looks like my letter made quite an impression."

Jessica winked in reply and rushed over to their brother. "Steven, are you OK?" she asked, kneeling next to him.

"You don't look so good," Elizabeth added, hurrying after Jessica. She sat down on the couch to Steven's left.

"I'm OK," he said slowly without looking up. He waved the wrinkled letter in front of his face. "It's just that I found this letter from Lila stuck in the mailbox—and it's so weird."

"Weird?" Elizabeth echoed to prompt him.

"Weird," Steven repeated. He smoothed the paper and started to read.

"'I love you. . . . I can hardly wait until I finish high school and we can begin our lives together. . . . We'll travel to all sorts of exotic places and invite all the right people to our parties. . . . I know I can make you a celebrity among lawyers, more famous than F. Lee Bailey.'"

Steven stopped abruptly and grimaced. "A celebrity among lawyers? What a thing to say—as if I want to be some kind of superstar." He shook his head. "I can't believe how superficial Lila can be sometimes."

"Well, she's always been that way, Steven," Jessica said.

Steven gave a low whistle. "Plus she's practically got us engaged. Just yesterday we agreed to put off any thoughts about the future until we cleared Lila's name."

Elizabeth got up and walked to the bookcase. "I'm surprised you and Lila were talking about the future so soon," she said, trying to sound casual. "You haven't been seeing each other very long."

She glanced at Jessica and gave a slight nod.

"She's right," Jessica said hurriedly. "Lila's really moving fast."

Steven put the letter on the coffee table and threw up his hands. "That's what I think. We stopped at Shop & Hop for some sodas yesterday, and all of a sudden Lila went off on some strange tangent. She started spouting off about a little house full of dogs and babies."

"Are you serious?" Elizabeth gasped, trying to keep from smiling.

"Yes!" Steven spread out his arms and shrugged. "She practically had us walking down the aisle. We actually got into a fight about our future. It was unbelievable."

"Believe it." Jessica gave a short laugh. "I'm glad you're starting to see what Lila is really like."

Steven rubbed his hands over his face. "I told her to put those thoughts on hold, and it seemed like she agreed with me." He stabbed a finger at the letter. "Now this. It's like everything I said went in one ear and out the other."

Steven got up, crossed the room, and stared out the window. Elizabeth and Jessica exchanged smiles of satisfaction.

Elizabeth was surprised that in spite of feeling guilty for doing something underhanded, she was proud of herself too. She pushed the feeling into the background. After all, it wasn't as if she did this for fun. She wrote the letter to save her brother from a terrible fate—Lila Fowler.

Elizabeth turned and walked over to stand next to Steven. "You knew Billie for a long time before you started planning a future," Elizabeth said tentatively. "You had formed a bond, and you had a lot in common. Maybe you shouldn't have let her go so easily."

"I second that statement," Jessica said as she jumped to her feet. "Billie was the girl for you. Not Lila. I mean, Billie actually *liked* your dirty old T-shirts and jeans. If you ask me, you're better off without Lila." Jessica winked at Elizabeth and flounced out of the room.

Elizabeth watched Steven's shoulders sag a little. They must have struck a nerve talking about Billie.

"Steven, maybe you and Lila rushed into this," Elizabeth said. "You were rebounding from your breakup with Billie, and Lila had just broken up with Bo." Bo Creighton, Lila's long-distance boyfriend, had called to break up with Lila the night before the fire. "Maybe all the drama over the case has made you believe you have feelings for Lila when you really don't."

Steven whirled around. "That's not true," he said firmly. "My feelings for Lila are real, and I

100

think she's a great girl. And don't even start in on the fact that you think she's guilty."

Elizabeth took a step backward. "OK, OK," she said. "But look at the way she's planning your future—and it's not a future you want either. Maybe you should cool it with her. And while you're at it, maybe you should think about talking to Billie too. You meant a lot to each other."

"You're right," Steven said, turning to face Elizabeth.

"I am?" Elizabeth asked, surprised at his sudden change of heart. She felt a surge of hope. Maybe he had decided to call Billie. Maybe he was coming to his senses after all.

"Yes, you are," Steven said. "But it's *my* life. Stay out of it, Elizabeth."

Early Thursday evening, Jessica was striding briskly toward the Dairi Burger, feeling on top of the world.

A guy in a red convertible slowed down and gave Jessica a long look. She smiled and waved, happy that she'd decided to wear her new black minidress. It totally showed off her perfect California tan. She stopped and checked her reflection in a store window, flipping her hair over her right shoulder. *Of course I'm stopping traffic,* Jessica thought contentedly.

Although Jessica was more than aware of all the admiring glances, they weren't the reason she was in such a good mood. She had called Lila earlier and asked her to come to the Dairi Burger. Tucked into her canvas tote bag was a present that was part of her plan to accomplish two things at once—get Lila out of Steven's life and renew Jessica's relationship with her best friend.

All Lila's personal photographs had been destroyed on the night of the Fowler Crest fire. When Jessica realized how devastating it would be if she had lost all her own mementos, she had decided to cheer her friend up by making her a photo album. She had dug out tons of photos of her and Lila and the rest of their friends that dated all the way back to kindergarten. She had even mixed in a few photos she had found of Lila's family from her parents' wedding and other functions.

It's a work of art, Jessica thought proudly. She had carefully glued all the pictures to delicate gold paper and bound the pages with thick black tape. The book closed with a silver clasp.

Jessica planned to give Lila the album, get her all teary eyed over the fabulous times they'd had together, then steer the conversation toward "Steven's" vision of the future. *Or the future* I *made up for him,* Jessica thought with a giggle. Then Lila would realize that if she planned to stay with Steven, she would have to give up her entire way of life—the way of life that included all the great times depicted in the photo album.

A brilliant plan, Jessica thought as she pushed open the door of the Dairi Burger. *Who says Elizabeth is the smart one?* Excitedly she scanned the interior of the restaurant.

At first the only customers she saw were a couple who were paying a lot more attention to each other than to their burger deluxe platters. Then she spied Lila sitting in the last booth, hunched over a magazine.

From the distracted look on Lila's face and the halfhearted way she was turning the pages, Jessica could tell she wasn't really interested. Lila was the picture of loneliness.

Jessica felt a pang of sorrow for her former best friend. For a fleeting moment she thought she shouldn't bring up Steven at all. *Maybe we can talk about something else,* Jessica thought. *Something that will cheer her up and take her mind off what's been going on.* But a moment later her conscience was silenced.

Jessica drew herself up straighter and took a deep breath. She knew she had to keep Lila and

103

Steven apart no matter what. This particular couple was just *not* acceptable. And Steven and Lila were about to see that fact for themselves. She'd just give things a little push in the right direction. Swinging her bag at her side, Jessica sauntered over to Lila's booth.

"Hey, you!" Jessica called cheerfully.

Lila jumped a little, as if Jessica's voice had startled her out of a daydream.

"Hi, Jess," Lila said wearily. "How've you been?"

"Fabulous!" Jessica grinned as she slid into the booth and dropped her bag on the vinyl bench next to her. "I stopped at the mall on the way over and found the cutest bikini."

"Nice," Lila said tonelessly.

The smile vanished from Jessica's face. "I'll get straight to the point," she said as seriously as she could. "The reason I asked you to meet me here is to tell you that I'm sorry we fought, Lila. And I have a kind of peace offering." She reached into her tote, pulled out the photo album, and slid the book across the table.

Lila stared at the gift with a surprised and confused expression. She reached over and fumbled with the clasp, then slowly opened the cover. The first picture was an enlarged group shot of the whole SVH crowd from a party Lila had thrown a couple of months earlier. Lila's hands started to tremble as she studied the photo and the inscription Jessica had lettered so carefully. *Lila Fowler, this is your life!* was written in gold paint marker above the picture.

"Oh, Jess, thank you so much. This is amazing," she said in a hushed voice. She paged through the book, stopping every once in a while to take a closer look at the entries.

"I remember this!" Lila exclaimed, pointing at a picture of Jessica and Lila from the second grade. They were standing outside Fowler Crest in shorts and T-shirts, having a snowball fight in the fake snowstorm Lila's father had created in the backyard. "We had the best time that day!"

"Yeah." Jessica laughed along with her friend. "Until the snow melted fifteen minutes later."

"Snow has no chance in Sweet Valley!" Lila said with a giggle.

Jessica felt a rush of warm feelings as she saw her friend laugh for the first time in weeks.

"Keep going, Li," she urged. "Some of the best pictures are toward the end. It was really fun putting this thing together." Lila smiled and continued to flip through the pages.

Suddenly she stopped turning the pages and stared at one of the photos for a long time.

"What are you looking at?" Jessica asked, leaning

across the table to get a look at the upside-down photograph.

"It's of a bunch of us in your backyard, and Steven's with us," Lila said. "Look! There's Kimberly Haver. This must be from a Unicorn Club party back in seventh grade. To think he was there all this time and I didn't even know he was alive."

Jessica saw the perfect opportunity to start phase two of her plan. She swallowed hard. She'd come over here to drive another nail in the coffin of the relationship between Lila and Steven. But Lila was being so nice that it wasn't going to be easy to go through with it.

She forced herself to remember the sickening feeling she got when she caught Lila and Steven locked in a heated embrace in the Wakefields' kitchen. *Ugh!* Jessica fought off the urge to shudder. She had to continue with her plan.

"Let's not be mad at each other anymore, Lila," Jessica said soothingly. "You know, maybe I was wrong about you and Steven. Maybe you *are* perfect for each other."

Lila almost dropped her soda glass as she looked at Jessica in surprise. "Well, now that you mention it . . . ," she began.

Jessica didn't let her finish. "I'll bet you're just

the person Steven needs to help him get ahead in his career."

Lila sat up straighter, her eyes brightening with interest. "Do you really think so? I mean, I *do* think I could help him meet the right people and get into something really profitable."

Jessica tilted her head to one side and pretended to ponder Lila's words. She tried hard not to smile. This was going to be even easier than she'd thought.

"I was thinking more along the lines of standing behind him," Jessica said. "You know, cooking, ironing his shirts, taking his shoes to the repair shop. He'll need someone to take care of all those details when he's a successful lawyer."

Lila's mouth dropped open in horror, and Jessica almost burst out laughing. Instead she thoughtfully twisted a strand of silky blond hair around her finger.

"Of course," she continued, staring at the ceiling in false reflection, "you'll want to have kids right away. Steven wants a big family. The more the merrier, he always says."

Jessica grinned innocently at Lila and reached forward to grab her friend's soda. She took a self-satisfied slurp.

Lila's eyes narrowed in anger. "I don't cook or iron," she protested through clenched teeth. "I don't even know *how* to cook or iron. And I have no intention of having kids right away."

Standing up quickly, Lila bashed the table with her knee, causing the soda glass to bounce dangerously. She didn't even flinch.

"Lila!" Jessica said, replacing the glass on the table. "Where are you going?"

Lila gathered up her photo album and magazine and opened her purse. "This is for my soda and the tip," she said, throwing some money on the table. "Honestly! After all these years I thought you knew me pretty well. I guess you don't."

Jessica leaned back in her seat and put her hands behind her head as she watched Lila hurry away. Mission accomplished.

"Oh, yes, I do, Lila," she whispered mischievously. "I know you better than you know yourself."

Chapter 7

Elizabeth sighed contentedly and cuddled closer to Todd. They were sitting on the couch in the Wakefields' den with their history notebooks open on their laps, but Elizabeth's mind wasn't on studying. She turned slightly to look up into Todd's coffee-colored eyes, and her notebook tumbled to the floor.

Todd leaned over her and reached for the floor to pick up her notes, but Elizabeth playfully pushed him back in his seat and planted a big kiss on his lips.

"Forget the notebook," Elizabeth said, running her fingers through Todd's curly brown hair. She nuzzled his neck and traced a trail of kisses across his cheek. "We have more important things to do."

"I'm sorry," Todd said, his eyes dancing. "I must

be in the wrong house. Either that or you're an imposter and you've kidnapped the real Elizabeth Wakefield."

"I'm not allowed to skip studying for some quality cuddling time with the guy I love?" Elizabeth asked in mock indignation. She sat up and crossed her arms in front of her chest.

Todd laughed and pulled her to him. "You're right," he said huskily. "Who am I to judge?" He wrapped her up in his strong arms, and Elizabeth lost herself in a long, passionate kiss.

When they parted, she let out a spontaneous giggle.

"What's got you in such a good mood, Wakefield?" Todd asked, reaching over to brush a strand of blond hair behind her ear.

"Steven and Lila," Elizabeth said with a smile.

"Steven and Lila?" Todd repeated, his brow furrowing. "I thought you were hoping they would break up."

"That's just it," Elizabeth said happily. "I think they're finally realizing how wrong they are for each other. Those letters were a stroke of genius. . . ."

Elizabeth stopped abruptly and felt her face flame red. She hadn't intended to tell Todd about the little scheme she and Jessica had cooked up.

"What letters?" Todd asked lightly. He trailed a finger down Elizabeth's burning cheek.

"Oh, um, uh, nothing," Elizabeth stammered. This was one of the rare times she wished she was more like Jessica. Maintaining a poker face was not one of Elizabeth's special talents. "Where were we?" she improvised, pulling Todd in for another kiss.

This time when they parted, it was Todd's turn to laugh. "What's eating you, Liz?" he asked. "You look like you just killed your best friend."

"What do you mean?" Elizabeth exclaimed.

"Hey! It's just a figure of speech," Todd said, holding his hands up in surrender. "You just seem a little distracted all of a sudden."

"I'm fine," Elizabeth squeaked. "We should really start studying." She leaned over and quickly grabbed her notebook from the floor. Ditto sheets fluttered out, scattering in all directions.

Todd's eyes narrowed with suspicion. "Come on, Elizabeth," he said, taking her hand. "What's going on? Does this have something to do with Steven and Lila? You mentioned something about letters. . . ."

Elizabeth let out a long, defeated sigh and stared at their entwined fingers. Todd knew her too well. She just hoped he wouldn't be too disappointed in her when he found out about what she and Jessica had done.

"You're going to think I'm horrible," Elizabeth began, "but we did it for Steven's own good."

"Did what for Steven's own good?" Todd asked, eyeing her warily. "And who's 'we'?"

"Jessica and me," Elizabeth said quietly. "We, uh, well, we sort of forged some letters—one from Lila to Steven and one from Steven to Lila."

"What did these *sort of* forged letters say?" Todd asked, disentangling his fingers from hers. Elizabeth could tell Todd was already stunned. After all, forging was as bad as lying, and lying wasn't something Elizabeth did very often. She might as well just tell him everything.

"They were intended to scare both of them off," Elizabeth said, launching ahead bravely. "Steven's letter to Lila was all about how great a wife she would make, taking care of tons of children and looking after a tiny house. Lila's letter to Steven was all about how she would introduce him to all the right people and make sure he was a famous lawyer."

Todd's eyes widened in disbelief.

"Needless to say, they were both a little freaked out," Elizabeth finished. She looked up at Todd hopefully, but he seemed totally appalled.

"Elizabeth! What were you thinking?" Todd asked. "Did Jessica blackmail you into doing this or something?"

Suddenly Elizabeth felt defensive. What she had done was a little sneaky, but she had done it for Steven's happiness. She hadn't expected Todd to be proud of her, but he could at least try to see that her intentions were good.

"We were afraid that they wouldn't see how wrong they were for each other until it was too late," Elizabeth said earnestly. "Somebody had to do something."

"This isn't like you, Elizabeth," Todd said. "How would you feel if someone pulled this on us?"

Elizabeth took one look into Todd's soulful, confused eyes and her heart turned.

"Pretty lousy," she admitted after a moment. "But Todd, if those letters don't work, I can't promise you I won't try something else. I'm really worried about Steven."

"It's *his* life, Liz," Todd said, standing abruptly. He looked down at her as she sat stunned on the couch. "It's not your place to play games with it."

"Todd! Wait!" Elizabeth called as he snatched up his notebooks and backpack and stalked out of the room. "Why are you getting so mad?" She followed him out to the front door.

"I don't know," Todd said, turning to face her. He fixed her with a steely gaze. "It's just sometimes you do things that make me wonder if I really know you at all."

113

Elizabeth gasped and pulled back as if she'd been slapped. "Todd! Don't you understand? Lila has already cost Steven his job and maybe even his career. He could be heading for disaster if they stay together. Please try to understand."

Todd's eyes softened slightly, and he leaned forward to give Elizabeth a light kiss on her forehead. "I know you're doing what you think is best," Todd said, leaning back and looking into her eyes. "I just want you to be careful, or you may end up hurting more people than you help. Lying has a way of doing that, you know."

"I know," Elizabeth murmured. "But let *me* worry about that." She stood on her tiptoes and kissed Todd quickly on the cheek.

"I'll call you later. But think about what I said," Todd warned. As he turned to go, Elizabeth touched the back of Todd's neck gently, then closed the door behind him.

You may end up hurting more people than you help. Todd's words echoed in Elizabeth's mind as she walked slowly up the stairs. Elizabeth would normally agree with him that lying wasn't worth the trouble it caused, but she couldn't see how anyone would get hurt by what she and Jessica had done. Lila and Steven hadn't been together for very long, so they probably wouldn't even go through much

114

postbreakup withdrawal. They would both be better off in the end.

Elizabeth stopped at the top of the stairs. She could hear scuffing sounds coming from the end of the hall. Steven had been playing Nerf basketball all morning, and she couldn't believe he was still at it.

His door was slightly ajar, so she knocked and pushed it open.

"Hey, Liz," Steven greeted her without taking his eyes from the basketball hoop. He threw the foam basketball and missed, picked it up again, and made a basket.

"I wanted to apologize for the other day," Elizabeth said sincerely. Ever since Steven had blown up at her in the den, she had wanted to clear the air between them—even if she didn't plan on telling him about the real author of his letter from Lila. "I didn't mean to upset you with all that talk about Billie."

"It's already forgotten," Steven said happily. "Come on in."

Elizabeth sighed in relief and parked herself on Steven's plaid bedspread. She watched as he threw the ball through the hoop again and again without so much as a pause.

"How many hours have you been at this?" she asked.

Steven picked the basketball up off the floor and popped it through the hoop. "Oh, about four or five, I guess. Want to have a game?"

Elizabeth toyed with a button on the front of her pink-flowered T-shirt. "No, thanks," she answered. "Can I ask you a question?"

Steven paused before tossing the basketball and turned to look at her. "Uh-oh. If you have to ask me whether you can ask a question instead of just asking me the question, it's something big." He sat down on the bed beside Elizabeth and tossed the ball from one hand to the other. "What's up?"

Elizabeth leaned back, propping herself up on her elbows. "I was just wondering—I know you haven't been very social lately. You haven't even seen Lila in a couple of days. What's keeping you holed up in here like a hermit? Do you have something on your mind?"

Steven answered without hesitation. "The Fowler Crest case."

Elizabeth's eyes widened with surprise and apprehension when she heard his words. She sat up straight and searched Steven's face for a sign that he was joking. But he looked perfectly serious. Was her brother obsessed?

"You're still working on the case even though Garrison fired you over it?" Elizabeth asked incredulously.

116

"Yes," he replied. "I've found some new evidence. It's only a matter of time before I have the case sewn up tight."

"New evidence?" Elizabeth asked. "Evidence that clears Lila?"

"More like evidence that proves John Pfeifer guilty," Steven answered with a smile. "I'm going to make sure that loser finally gets locked away like he should have been a long time ago."

A cold chill ran down Elizabeth's spine. Steven seemed pretty convinced of John's guilt. She wasn't sure what this new evidence was, but if Steven was right about John, that meant that Elizabeth had been working alongside a complete maniac at the *Oracle*.

"I just wish I could get inside Pfeifer's house," Steven said, rubbing his chin. "I'm sure I'd find something solid there that would prove my theory."

"Steven!" Elizabeth exclaimed. "You're not actually thinking about breaking into John's house, are you? I mean, it was bad enough when you went through his desk. What if the D.A. found out?"

"Of course I'm not going to break into his house, Liz," Steven answered evenly. "But Garrison can't prevent me from investigating on my own. I believe Lila is innocent, and I'm going to prove it."

Steven got up and started playing again.

"It's strange, but doing this helps me think," he said. "I know I'm missing one piece of the puzzle, and when I find it, I'm bringing my evidence to the D.A."

Elizabeth sighed. She knew that her brother was determined, and it was useless to argue anymore. It looked like nothing was going to stop him now.

Jessica slammed the front door and bounded up the stairs. No doubt Elizabeth was sitting up in her room doing something boring like studying or working on a crossword puzzle, and Jessica couldn't wait to tell her the good news about her meeting with Lila. She burst into her sister's room and found her, predictably, sitting at her desk.

"Aren't you going to say hello to your better half?" Jessica asked breezily.

"Hello," Elizabeth answered without looking up from her chemistry book. "Ever hear of knocking?"

Jessica was in too good a mood to respond to Elizabeth's comment. "How can you sit up here studying on this beautiful afternoon?" Without waiting for an answer, Jessica dumped the blue bikini onto the bed. "Look what I bought. Isn't it great?"

Elizabeth put down her book and groaned. "*More* clothes? Didn't you get enough on your shopping expeditions with Lila?"

Jessica made an exasperated face. "I didn't get a new *bathing suit*. Don't you just love it?"

"It's nice," Elizabeth said halfheartedly.

"Maybe you'll be more interested in the conversation I just had with Lila," Jessica announced, stuffing the bikini back in the bag. She almost laughed when she saw the spark of curiosity in her sister's eyes.

"What conversation?" Elizabeth asked. She was pretending to be bored, but Jessica could see right through her sister's little act. The girl was hanging on Jessica's every word.

She flashed Elizabeth a mischievous smile, then quickly filled her twin in on what had happened at the Dairi Burger. "The relationship between Steven and Lila is on its way to ruin."

"I hope you're right," Elizabeth said. "But Steven says he's been thinking about the Fowler Crest case all day. He still won't leave it alone. He's totally convinced that John Pfeifer is the arsonist."

Jessica shuddered. "It wouldn't surprise me one bit if that creep turned out to be guilty," she said. "Maybe Steven's right. Then he'll prove Lila's innocent *and* break up with her. And everything will be back to normal!"

"I hope you're right," Elizabeth said. "But there's just one thing bothering me."

Jessica rolled her eyes. Why couldn't Elizabeth ever just be happy? "What now?"

"Well, Steven hasn't seen Lila in a few days, and from what you said about your conversation with her, Lila won't be going anywhere near Steven in the near future," Elizabeth answered.

"That's what we *wanted,* silly!" Jessica said, bounding off the bed and crossing the room to Elizabeth's mirror. She grabbed a little tub of lip balm off her sister's desk. "What's the problem?"

"Ever hear of absence making the heart grow fonder?" Elizabeth asked. She got up from her desk and plopped down on the edge of her bed. "What if they both suddenly realize they miss each other?"

Jessica flipped her hair over her shoulders and dabbed at her lips. She had to admit, her sister had a point.

"So let's not give them time to miss each other." She turned around to face Elizabeth, another brilliant idea quickly taking form.

"I think we ought to strike while the iron is hot," Jessica continued. "If we can get them alone together soon, while Steven is still put off by the letter and Lila is horrified about cooking and ironing, I'll bet there would be a huge blowup."

Elizabeth nodded solemnly. "Right. Let's not give Lila time to forget about the idea of washing

Steven's socks. But how can we get them together?"

Jessica jumped onto the bed next to Elizabeth and curled her legs under her. "I know what to do!" she said excitedly. "It's perfect. The Big Mesa game is Saturday, right?"

Elizabeth's eyes clouded with confusion. "What does football have to do with this?" she asked.

Jessica grinned. Sometimes her dear sister could be *so* dense. "It's a big game," she said, bouncing up and down a couple of times for emphasis. "We'll make sure Lila goes, and I'll tell her Steven wants to meet her to talk somewhere off by themselves. Meanwhile you can get Steven to go to the game with you and Todd and then tell him Lila wants to see him."

Elizabeth stared at Jessica, looking half impressed, half shocked. "I knew you had a devious mind, Jessica," she said jokingly. "But don't you think this is a little over the top? I mean, once they got together, wouldn't they figure it out?"

"Oh, they'll be so busy breaking up, they won't think to ask each other how they got there!" Jessica exclaimed. "It's *perfect*, Liz!"

Elizabeth sighed, but then Jessica saw her sister's mouth start to turn up in a reluctant smile. With Elizabeth's help, Jessica's plan was sure to work. Steven and Lila's relationship was about to go up in smoke!

❖ ❖ ❖

Devon gave the squeaky hinge another drop of oil, then swung the kitchen door back and forth. It moved smoothly and silently. Satisfied, he put the oilcan down on the counter and wiped his hands on a rag. The noise had been driving him crazy.

In the past couple of days Devon had noticed that there were lots of repairs that needed doing around Nana's house. Leaky faucets needed washers, light switches needed rewiring, and drains needed fixing. Luckily when Devon was young, he used to hang out with any plumbers, electricians, and cable guys who came by the mansion. It was a way out of boredom, and it had taught him a few things as well.

Devon walked into the kitchen and started washing his hands in the sink. He smiled as he remembered what Nana had said to him the night before when she had caught him working on an old clock.

"You don't have to do that," she'd told him. "Ride around on your motorcycle and get to know the town; go to the beach and meet some girls."

Devon had told her there would be plenty of time for that. He enjoyed making himself useful. Nana had provided him with a place to stay, and he didn't want to just lie around taking up space. Besides, working with his hands kept his mind occupied too. It helped him deal with the war between logic and emotion that was going on inside him.

Devon sighed, shook the water from his hands, and plopped down at the kitchen table. The longer he stayed in Nana's house, the more he wanted to give in to her apparent kindness. It was hard to feel anything but affection and admiration for this woman who appeared to spread goodness wherever she went.

At the same time Devon struggled harder and harder to keep a hold on his heart. What if her kindness was just greed in disguise?

Devon noticed a framed print on the floor, propped up against the wall. There was a tiny hole in the wall above it that looked as if it had once held a nail. Devon shook his head. Maybe he would rehang the artwork, and that would be his last chore for the day. He headed for the garage to find a nail and hammer.

The small, musty garage was in an even worse state than the house. There were shelves along one wall where Nana stored everything from canned food and broken lamps to the few tools she owned. The shelves themselves were cracked and broken. Devon made a mental note to replace them as soon as he could borrow Nana's car.

Devon started rummaging around, looking for a box of nails. Suddenly one of the shelves gave and a metal box came tumbling down. Devon jumped back just in time to avoid being hit on the head.

"That was close," he muttered as the box crashed to the floor. When it hit, the top flew open and the contents of the box spilled out on the dirty cement.

Devon blinked at the mess. There were letters—dozens of them—in envelopes of cream, pale yellow, pastel blue, and pink. *Wow*, Devon thought, *Nana must be really sentimental if she saved all her correspondence.* He bent down to scoop the envelopes into the box.

As Devon grabbed up one of the letters he couldn't help peeking at the address. Maybe they were secret love letters from Nana to some long lost boyfriend. But when he saw the carefully printed address, Devon's heart nearly stopped.

The letter was addressed to Devon himself at his house in Connecticut. Return to Sender was stamped across the front of the sealed envelope in huge red letters.

Devon's hands trembled as he picked up another letter, then another and another. His mind reeled as he saw his own name printed again and again. Some were brittle and yellowed with age and the ink had smudged on a few of them, but they were all undeniably addressed to him, and all were stamped Return to Sender. Devon's heart thudded in his chest, and sweat broke out on his palms. The whole pile of letters had been sent to him in Connecticut, but he had never received a single one. His parents must have intercepted them and returned them all unopened.

"How could they do this to me?" Devon whispered. "How could they make me think that Nana didn't care about me?" Numb, he stuffed the envelopes back into the metal box and carried it into the house, through the living room, and into the tiny space that had been his bedroom for the past few days.

He plopped down on his bed and dumped the contents of the box out onto the patchwork quilt. Then he just sat there and stared.

Should I open them? he wondered hesitantly. For a moment he felt like he was invading Nana's privacy.

"But they *are* addressed to me," he said out loud.

Nervously Devon wiped his palm on the thigh of his jeans and plucked a cream-colored envelope from the top of the pile. He held the envelope carefully and examined the postmark. The letter had been written nearly a year after Nana had left the Whitelaws'. He slid his finger under the flap and tore along the crease. He swallowed, then pulled out several pages and began to read.

❖   ❖   ❖

125

My Dearest Devon,

Did you get the trains I sent you for your birthday? I hope you are enjoying playing with them. Maybe you can come to visit me someday soon, and together we'll take a ride on a real train.

Blood rushed to Devon's head, and he felt as if he might explode with anger. *I wonder what they did with those trains,* Devon thought. *They probably just trashed them.* It would be nice to think that his parents had at least donated the gift to a charity, but he knew better. They never thought of anyone but themselves.

"And these letters prove that," Devon whispered through clenched teeth.

He picked up another envelope and tore it open. *Dearest Devon,* he read, *I always think of you at Christmas. . . .*

Working frantically as if drawn by a force he couldn't control, Devon ripped open envelope after envelope. He read a few lines each time before putting the letter aside to grab another.

Finally Devon reached the last, a heavy envelope of pastel blue. It was dated only a month earlier. Devon held the letter carefully, almost afraid to believe that she had been so devoted all this time. He tore it open and read.

*　　*　　*

Dear Devon,
I know you'll be going to your junior prom soon. You must be so grown up now.

Devon's arm dropped. He was too overcome with emotion to go on. He rested his head in his hands, exhausted. Piled beside him were years of Nana's affection. Of her longing to see him. Of her caring. Years and years during which Devon had made himself forget about her. Years and years in which his parents had been so distant—so cold. He had longed for Nana all that time and had been tremendously hurt when he hadn't heard from her.

All the pain Devon had felt as a sad and lonely child welled up inside. He had locked it away for so long, and now it threatened to overwhelm him.

Devon took a deep breath and a harsh, rasping sound tore through his chest. Soon his whole body was racked with wave after wave of powerful dry sobs. Devon doubled over and hugged his arms to his body. Then, when he thought he could stand the pain no longer, he finally wept.

Chapter 8

Devon lay flat on his back with his forearm covering his eyes. He took a deep breath and let it out slowly, wondering how long he had been crying. Sitting up, he blinked a few times to clear any remnants of tears and stared out the window. It looked as if the sun was just setting.

Stretching out his arms, Devon smiled slightly. The outpouring of emotion had left him feeling drained and weak, yet somehow refreshed too. The strain of holding his sadness inside was gone, and his whole body felt freer, lighter.

Now he could do what he really wanted to do— read each and every letter all the way through. Devon picked a letter at random, leaned back against the headboard, and started to read.

Devon perused each letter carefully, letting the

words wrap around him like a warm blanket. The more he read, the closer he felt to Nana and the more certain he was that he had finally found someone he could really trust. Her love and caring poured from every page. He was so absorbed that he didn't hear the door click open. He didn't even know someone else was in the room with him until Nana spoke.

"Devon," she said softly.

A single look at Nana's face told Devon that she already understood what had happened. Their eyes locked for a moment—a moment of deep communication.

Devon began gathering the letters into a neat pile. "All these letters, all those years," he said hoarsely. "When I asked you why you never tried to contact me, why didn't you tell me?" He picked up one of the envelopes. "It would have meant so much to me to know."

Nana sat down on the edge of the bed and clasped her hands in the lap of her long blue skirt. She was still wearing the name tag she wore at the day care center on the right side of her crisp white blouse.

"Your parents' deaths are so fresh, Devon," Nana said softly, shaking her head. "I thought it was enough for you to bear. I was afraid if I told you about the letters, it would . . . complicate things." Nana's eyes glistened. "I didn't want you to hate your parents."

Devon's lip curled. "I think that was decided

129

long before I arrived on your doorstep," he said, his voice full of cold rage. "Why did they keep sending your letters back?"

Nana stood and walked to the window. She stared out silently for a few moments before turning back to Devon.

"Well?" Devon prompted.

Nana twisted her hands. "Because . . . I suppose they . . ." Her voice trailed off.

Devon snorted. "They knew how heartbroken I was about never hearing from you. I asked about you all the time." His voice cracked. "When I was little, I cried about you every night. Then when I was older, something inside of me just closed up. You were more like my mother than my mother, and you were gone forever."

Nana turned and put her hand on Devon's shoulder. "Oh, no, Devon," she said. "You mustn't feel that way. Your mother loved you very much."

"That's a laugh," Devon said dryly.

"Listen to me, Devon," Nana said. "She loved you the only way she knew how. She had a hard time expressing her love, that's all." Her voice dropped to a whisper. "I think it hurt her sometimes that you and I became so close. I think she felt left out."

"Left out?" Devon snorted again. "I used to ache for my mother to give me a hug, or play with me, or do one single thing to show me she loved me."

He stood up and started to pace the small area between his bed and his closet. "But all she did was ignore me or criticize me. You were the one who bathed me, who fed me, who took care of me when I was sick. If she loved me so much, why didn't she do those things?"

Nana's face crumpled a little. "I'm sure she would have if she had known how, Devon. Maybe your mother just wasn't good at showing affection."

Devon spoke through gritted teeth. "I'll say she wasn't. Besides, she was too busy going to society parties. Having a little boy around was always so inconvenient."

"Devon, please don't talk this way," Nana begged.

But Devon barely heard her.

"Do you remember the time I fell and skinned my knee in the yard?" he demanded. "I ran into the house, crying for my mother." His face darkened with anger. "That was before I knew better," Devon rambled on. "She was getting ready to go out, and she didn't want my muddy hands on her dress. She screamed at you to get me away from her." Devon clenched his hands into fists at his sides. "My father was even worse—always trying to control me but never trying to love me. Never playing ball with me or going places with me the way other dads did. I *do* hate them. I hate them, and I'll never, ever forgive them."

"Devon, please sit down." She walked over to him and led him back to the bed. "What you're doing can only hurt you more. Hate is never the answer. You've got to put it behind you if you're ever to get on with living."

Devon let her words sink in. In his heart he knew she was right. The longer he carried this bitterness with him, the more it would eat away at his soul, the way it had been eating at him since his parents had died.

"I'll try not to hate them," he said finally. "I'll take it day by day."

Nana patted his hand. "That's the spirit." She paused for a moment.

"There's something I've been thinking about very seriously, Devon," she said. "I know it's a big step, but I wish you would consider staying on with me. There is an excellent high school here, and I think you should get back to your studies before you miss much more. Not that catching up will be a problem for a brilliant boy like you," she added.

Devon felt calmness and warmth slowly flooding his body. *Staying here in Sweet Valley would be a dream come true,* he thought. He suddenly realized how much he missed going to school and studying science, being around kids his own age.

"What do you say, Devon?" Nana asked. "Will you give it a try?"

Devon looked into Nana's kind blue eyes. Nana was the only person he had ever trusted, and now he knew he still could.

"I'd love to stay," he said finally. For the first time since he could remember, he really felt as if he had found a home. "I hope that eventually you'll agree to become my legal guardian."

Nana's voice shook with emotion. "Of course, Devon. If that's what you decide you want, nothing would please me more."

"It is what I want," Devon said, surprised at his own certainty. He opened his mouth to tell Nana about the inheritance but swallowed the words. He didn't want talk of money to spoil this moment, and he knew Nana wouldn't care anyway. There would be time enough to discuss it. Now that he had found a home, he had all the time in the world.

"Mind if I sit down?" Jessica asked brightly. It was Friday afternoon, and Jessica had spotted Lila eating alone in the cafeteria. It was time to put the last phase of Operation Breakup in motion.

"Huh?" Lila asked, obviously startled. "No, go ahead."

Jessica plopped into a chair and watched as Lila listlessly pushed her food around on her plate.

"Listen, Li, I know you're worried about your

133

hearing, and you've been through a lot lately. But it's time for you to snap out of this depression you've been in."

Lila's lips curved into a half smile. "Thanks, Jess, but it's easier said than done." She sat up straighter. "Actually, I have been feeling a *little* better lately. They've done a lot of construction on the house. The sooner I see it fully restored, the quicker I can put the fire out of my mind."

"That's great," Jessica said sincerely. She took a bite of her tuna salad sandwich and washed it down with a swig of water.

"Of course," Lila said, "I'll never entirely forget what happened."

"Maybe not," Jessica said cheerfully, "but once you get back into the swing of things, you'll brighten right up."

"What do you mean, 'get back into the swing of things'?" Lila asked, looking wary.

"You've got to start getting out more," Jessica responded. "The big football game against Big Mesa is tomorrow. Why don't you come with me? It'll be like old times."

Lila's eyes widened. "Oh, I don't know if I'm up for the football game, Jess. Everyone will be staring at me."

"Hiding won't help," Jessica said firmly. "The sooner people get used to seeing you out, the quicker they'll stop staring. You never know, Lila. You might just have fun."

Jessica held her breath. If Lila didn't agree to come with her, her plan was as good as finished.

Lila sighed. "Well, I guess it might be a good idea for me to get out," she said finally.

"You won't regret it, Lila," Jessica gushed. She could hardly contain her joy. Operation Breakup was nearly complete!

Steven scuffed his toe in the dirt as he watched the crowd gather in the bleachers before the Big Mesa football game. His eyes scanned the field.

"Excuse me." He heard a feminine voice behind him. Steven moved aside to let a pretty brunette girl pass. She started making her way up the bleachers toward a gangly guy who was waving enthusiastically. The girl wrapped her arms around the boy's neck and kissed him gently on the cheek. Steven gazed at them and felt a pang of nostalgia for Billie.

Sighing, Steven wished for a moment that he was still in high school and could start all over again. *Compared to what's going on in my life now, I'd take those days in a minute,* he thought.

He checked his watch and realized he was running late. Gathering up his hot dog wrapper and empty soda cup, Steven started to make his way down the bleachers. The crowd erupted into wild cheers and applause just as Steven dumped his trash in a garbage can. He looked up to see that Ken Matthews, the SVH quarterback, had just scrambled for a touchdown. The whole team was congratulating him in the end zone.

Steven's shoulders slumped as he turned to head for the school building. For an odd moment he wanted to be Ken—to feel that sense of elation and total confidence. Right now Matthews didn't have a care in the world.

Steven felt as if he had the weight of ten worlds on his shoulders. He had spent hours now trying to figure out what his next step should be in investigating the Fowler Crest case. He wished for the hundredth time that he had been able to convince the D.A. that John Pfeifer was worth investigating. Steven was sure that if he could just get a look around John's room, he would find something that would link him undeniably to the fires. But only the police could get a legal warrant to search someone's house. Steven kicked at a small stone in frustration.

As he approached the back door of the school, his chest felt hollow and his stomach was queasy. Moments ago Elizabeth had told him that Lila wanted to meet him by the bathrooms. She'd said it was important. It had been days since Steven had seen Lila. The letter she had sent about their future together had really made him think. He had to tell Lila that it was over. They just didn't want the same things.

The problem was, Steven hadn't really figured out how to handle it yet. He had been biding his time, trying to come up with a gentle way to break it to Lila, but now it looked like he was going to have to face the music before he was ready.

Steven took a deep breath as he pulled open the door. Everything in him wished that he could ditch this meeting with Lila. At the same time he knew he couldn't keep avoiding her forever, particularly since he was still working on her case.

Steven bit his lip as he headed down the main corridor toward the bathrooms. With every step his heart sank a little further. *Please don't make a scene, Lila,* he prayed. *And for heaven's sake, don't cry.*

Lila sighed as she leaned against the wall outside the ladies' room. Any minute now Steven would come around the corner. *He of the little house and barbecue grill,* Lila thought, curling her lip. *What on earth will I do if he suggests a date—or tries to kiss me?*

Lila folded her arms and stared at the floor. She wanted nothing more than to run away, to get on a plane and head for some tropical island. She watched a couple pass, laughing and swinging their clasped hands. She longed to be as carefree as they were.

I can't even leave town until I'm cleared of

charges, so the tropical island is out, she thought wistfully. *Steven is the only one who truly believes in me and will help me clear myself of charges. I have to be grateful to him for that, no matter what I think of his idea of the perfect future.*

Still, Lila knew it was time to tell Steven how she felt. It wouldn't be fair to stay with him any longer. Jessica had been right all along—she and Steven were a horrible mismatch. Lila only hoped he wouldn't be so angry and hurt that he would drop her case. She still needed his help.

Lila looked up and saw a figure advancing toward her. There was no mistaking the way those broad shoulders swung slightly when he walked, the way his head was held high, and that slightly defiant thrust of his chin. The moment of reckoning with Steven had finally come. Lila twisted her hands as the knot in her stomach tightened.

Chapter 9

Devon decided to finally take Nana's advice and explore Sweet Valley on his Harley. Now that he was sure he would be staying on here, it was time to really get to know the town. He let the front door close behind him and took a deep breath of the warm, balmy air. He smiled—possibly the first purely content smile of his entire life.

"Sweet Valley, here I come," Devon whispered as he pulled on his helmet and secured the chin strap. He swung himself onto the bike and revved the engine, grinning at the roar of the motor. Looking back up at the house, he saw Nana waving from the doorway. Devon lifted his hand and then took off, knowing for the first time in what seemed like ages that he had a place he wanted to come back to.

At the end of the quaint street where Nana lived,

Devon turned toward town. He had seen a few cool-looking burger joints and even a bike shop when he had first arrived, but he hadn't wanted to take the time to stop. Now he had all the time in the world.

I'm going to have a life here, he thought with a giddy sense of anticipation. Nana had made his dream come true for him.

Devon stopped at a red light and placed his feet on the ground for balance. Looking around, he noticed a couple of guys and girls tossing a football back and forth on the lawn in front of a large white house. They appeared to be about Devon's age, and all of them were tan. Devon turned his arm and studied his own pale skin. *I'm going to have to catch some serious rays if I'm going to fit in here,* Devon realized.

He gave the group a long look, studying each of their smiling faces. *Will these kids be my friends?* he wondered. He couldn't imagine actually fitting in—a cold climate East Coaster in this mellow, warm place. But maybe, just maybe, he'd make a few real friends here, people who cared about more than his money and good looks.

The light turned green, and Devon hit the accelerator. Two blocks later he was in the heart of Sweet Valley's business district. Devon noticed one of the diners he had seen on his first day in town and pulled up just before the parking lot to take a look.

"Dairi Burger," Devon read with a smirk. "How

quaint." He pulled off his helmet and watched as a hoard of kids poured out of the diner. They were all dressed in red and white, and they laughed and shouted as they piled into a big, forest green Ford Explorer. As the car pulled away, one of the girls stuck a pom-pom out the window and yelled, "Go, Gladiators!"

"Gladiators?" Devon said aloud. Then he noticed the huge sign in the window of the Dairi Burger. It read Go Sweet Valley High! Beat Big Mesa!

So that's what all the hoopla was about. A football game. *They must be headed for the high school,* Devon thought. A tingle of nervousness shot down his spine. *My new school.* On the spur of the moment he decided to follow the Explorer. In a few days he would register for classes at SVH. He was about to get a glimpse of his future.

Steven listened to his footsteps echoing down the hall as he walked toward Lila. She was leaning with her shoulder up against the wall, and her face was in shadow.

There was a thick, heavy lump of dread in Steven's chest. Lila looked so frail and alone. How was he going to tell her that he thought they should break up?

The second half of the game was about to kick off, and the hallways had emptied. As Steven leaned on the wall facing Lila the school was a vacuum of silence.

141

"Hello, Lila," Steven said quietly.

"Hi." Lila gave him a tight little smile. Steven watched as she shifted from one foot to the other. Her eyes were trained at the floor.

She must be feeling uncomfortable because she hasn't heard from me, Steven figured. He decided the only gentlemanly thing to do was to try to lighten the mood.

"How's it going?" Although Steven tried for a light, easy tone, his voice came out brittle. *Not a good start,* Steven thought.

"It's going just fine," Lila answered, "considering I'm the number-one criminal in Sweet Valley and my house is a wreck and my parents are AWOL and some psycho is out to get me." Lila actually started to laugh, easing the tension slightly. "How's everything going with you, Steven?"

Steven grinned. "Couldn't be better. I lost my job, and the D.A.'s office thinks I'm an accessory to a crime. Oh, yeah—since I didn't finish my internship, I'll probably flunk out this semester. How could anyone top that?"

The two of them cracked up. "Great team, aren't we?" Steven said after a moment. "I think we've been good for each other, don't you?"

Lila took a deep breath. "Steven, about us being a great team—when the whole business with the fire and my arrest happened, I was desperate

142

for a friend, and you were there. I can't tell you how much it meant to me."

Lila looked into Steven's eyes for a moment, and he felt a quick, sharp pang in his heart. He was painfully aware of her beauty and the fact that she still relied on him. More than anything, he still wanted to protect her.

Steven felt his sense of dread start to grow. The poor girl had fallen so hard for him.

But we just aren't right for each other, Steven told himself firmly. He still cared for her, and he fully intended to clear her name, but leading her on would be cruel.

He was just going to have to let her down easily.

Well, here goes nothing. "Lila, I—"

"Wait, Steven," Lila interrupted. "Let me finish." She looked into his eyes for a moment, then looked away.

"When we met, I was on the rebound from Bo, and you were on the rebound from Billie." She touched Steven's arm gently. "Then we found each other."

Steven swallowed. Where was she going with this?

"Without your support," Lila continued earnestly, "I don't think I could have gotten through the last few weeks. Knowing you believed in me gave me strength."

The knot in Steven's stomach twisted again. "I still believe you're innocent, Lila," he said miserably.

He was feeling worse and worse. The girl had given him her heart, and now he'd have to break it. He despised the thought of hurting her.

"Lila, I don't know how to tell you this . . . ," he began.

"Stop!" Lila said sharply. "I'm sorry, Steven, but I think we got into this too fast. We needed each other for the wrong reasons." Lila shrugged. "I think we got involved before we really knew each other. We're really not anything alike. I'm attracted to you, but it would never work in the long run. Please try to understand."

Steven's heart raced. He didn't know whether to be shocked or psyched.

"Huh?" he blurted. "Are you saying you don't want to see me anymore?"

Lila's shoulders sagged. "I feel terrible, but it's the best thing. It really is. The life you want is different from the life I want. I'm sorry. You've been so good to me. I hate to hurt you."

Steven searched for something to say, but the first thing that came to mind was "hooray!" Somehow it just didn't seem like the right sentiment for the moment.

When Lila looked at Steven, her eyes were glistening with tears. "I guess I noticed our differences, but I never really thought about them until I read that letter you left in my locker."

"Letter?" Steven whispered. What was she talking about?

"I'm flattered that you care for me so much," Lila continued, as if she hadn't heard him. "You'll get over it, though understandably it will probably take some time."

"Um, Lila?" Steven attempted to interrupt, but she just kept going.

"I mean, when I read how you can't wait for us to have a little house full of babies and dogs, I knew we were all wrong for each other—"

"Lila!" Steven blurted. She stopped short and stared at him wide-eyed, as if she couldn't believe that he'd dare interrupt her. Steven's eyes narrowed. "What letter are you talking about?" he asked.

Lila blinked rapidly. "What do you mean, what letter? I'm talking about the letter you left in my locker a few days ago. The one where you said you couldn't wait until I finished high school so we could be together. The one that talked about backyard barbecues and measly little D.A. salaries."

Steven knitted his brows. "The only letter I know of is the one you left in my mailbox," he said slowly.

"Huh?" Now Lila was obviously confused.

"You were the one who said you couldn't wait until you finished high school so we could be together," Steven reminded her. "You talked about the places we'd go and the parties we'd give. You

145

laid out our whole future. Frankly, Lila, it sounded like you had us walking down the aisle."

"I don't get it," Lila said. "I never sent you a letter. Are you playing some kind of game with me?"

"No game." Steven reached into the pocket of his jacket and pulled out the folded letter. "I was going to give this back to you." He handed it to Lila.

Lila held the paper between two fingers and studied it as if it were a biology lab specimen.

"This stationery is so cheap!" Lila exclaimed. "I would never buy anything like this."

She popped open her purse and pulled out another letter, which she handed over to Steven. "It just so happens I was going to give this back to you."

Each of them unfolded their sheet of paper and began to read. A moment later they looked at each other openmouthed.

"I never wrote this," Lila sputtered.

"I figured you didn't," Steven said. He stood next to Lila and looked over her shoulder, holding his letter next to hers. Immediately he knew for sure they'd been had, and he had a feeling he knew who was behind the scheme.

"Check it out," Steven said. "Both letters were printed on a computer. And don't you think it's a little strange that our signatures are so similar?"

Lila studied the bottoms of the letters.

"I don't believe I didn't notice it before!" Lila

exclaimed suddenly. "That's *Jessica's* handwriting. No guy would ever write like that. She might as well have dotted the *i* with a little heart!"

An angry blush was rising on Lila's cheeks, and Steven had to swallow a laugh.

"Take it easy, Lila," Steven said, placing his hands on her shoulders and forcing her to look at him. "And don't just blame Jessica either. I have a feeling that both of them were in on this."

"You think *Liz* would do something this dishonest?" Lila asked incredulously.

"Think about it," Steven said. "She is the writer in the family."

"Well, if she did, Jessica definitely talked her into it." Lila took a deep breath. "And to think that girl had me convinced she wanted to be friends again."

"She probably does," Steven said with a smile. "She just has a bizarre way of showing it."

"True," Lila said. "That's Jessica, I guess." She let out a slight giggle.

Steven was glad the mood had lightened again. They still had some unfinished business to take care of.

"Lila, about what you were saying before . . . ," Steven said tentatively.

"Oh, Steven," Lila said. "Liz and Jessica were right about one thing—we *are* completely wrong for each other. I mean, we could have written these letters."

Steven chuckled. "You're right," he said, glancing

at the one signed from him. "Except for this part about me wanting a white picket fence. They know I'm not *that* cheesy."

"And who on earth is F. Lee Bailey anyway?" Lila asked, glancing at her own letter in confusion. Steven clapped a hand over his mouth to keep from cracking up.

"What?" Lila demanded indignantly. "Am I supposed to know who he is?"

"Never mind," Steven said between fits of laughter.

"Well, maybe I'll just wash my hands of all you Wakefield people," Lila said, placing her hands on her hips. "I cannot believe that Jessica did this to me."

Steven controlled his laughter and looked Lila in the eyes. The girl had a right to be mad, and come to think of it, so did he. Even though his darling sisters had turned out to be right about him and Lila, where did they get off messing around in his love life?

"You know what?" Steven said, wrapping a friendly arm around Lila's slim shoulders. "You're not the only one who's been duped here. The question is, what are we going to do about it?"

"Why, Steven Wakefield," Lila purred jokingly, "are we talking about revenge?"

"With a capital *R*," Steven answered.

Chapter 10

Devon could hear the rousing beat of the marching band as he walked behind the crowd of kids from the Explorer. A girl with straight red hair kept turning around to check him out, so Devon kept his hands stuffed in his pockets and his eyes trained on the field. He didn't want to catch her eye because she looked like the bubbly type who might introduce herself and demand information. Right now Devon just wanted to blend in.

As he approached the field Devon could see a line of majorettes prancing off toward the sidelines, waving to the crowd. *I guess it's nice to know some things never change,* he thought. *Just as long as it's not* all *the same.*

He glanced at the scoreboard and noticed there were a couple of minutes left before the second half began. While he was debating whether he should join the crowd in the stands or find a less cramped place to take in the game, two little kids ran by him carrying hot dogs and sodas. Devon's stomach rumbled. *First things first,* he thought. He turned and headed for the concession stand.

As he joined the line he listened to the fragments of conversation around him.

"I can't believe she actually wore it!"

"It's the coolest set of wheels."

"You're kidding."

"So then I said to him . . ."

"No way! You *must* be kidding."

It had been a long time since he'd been surrounded by such easy conversation. Devon felt his shoulders start to relax as he inched forward in line.

After ordering, Devon carried his hot dog and drink down to the sidelines, away from the bleachers. There were a few other people standing there who, for the most part, looked like reporters and photographers. Devon fit right in with them. He had grown used to being an observer during the past few weeks and figured he'd be joining the rest of the students soon enough—Monday, in fact.

A huge roar went up from the home bleachers as the Gladiators took the field. Devon decided to trash his empty can and napkin before the game got started, and he looked around for a trash can.

As he turned, a flash of blond hair caught his eye, and Devon's heart stopped. He was looking at the most beautiful girl he had ever seen.

She looks like an angel, Devon thought. She was wearing a pale yellow sundress and was laughing as she talked to a friend. Devon followed her with his eyes as she climbed the steps to the bleachers.

It wasn't just her beauty that kept Devon's attention as she wove her way through the crowd, waving to various people. She looked so sweet and pure and natural—exactly Devon's type.

Half dazed, Devon slowly started to walk toward the stands. He couldn't lose this girl in the crowd before he found out who she was. He was just about to start up the steps when two insanely huge guys in varsity basketball jackets stepped in front of him, blocking his view. Devon craned his neck and caught a final, fleeting glimpse of the girl's beautiful hair before she vanished from view completely.

With a sigh of regret Devon sat down at the far end of the bleachers. But he knew all was not lost. This school didn't seem to be that big. He would just track her down on Monday and find out everything he could about her.

Devon looked at the smiling couples he saw all around him. He couldn't even remember the last time he'd been on a date. Finding a girlfriend had never been first on his priority list.

Devon furrowed his brow. Most of the girls back home had only been interested in his looks and his money. A picture of the girl in the pale yellow dress flashed before his mind's eye. She had seemed so natural and carefree. Surely she wasn't as superficial as the Connecticut society girls he had come in contact with.

A rowdy group of younger kids crowded into the space next to him, and Devon began to feel closed in. He stood and started to wander along the sidelines. He glanced over his shoulder one last time to see if he could catch another glimpse of the blond girl. His heart was still pounding from the sight of her, and his palms were even sweating. But there was no finding her among the sea of faces.

"Give me a *G!*"

Devon was startled by a cheer rising up from the track around the football field. He glanced over at the cheerleaders as the fans responded enthusiastically. There were a bunch of beautiful girls bouncing around in red-and-white miniskirts. Devon scanned them quickly. Not bad, but none of them could compare to . . . wait a minute.

One of the two girls cheering her heart out in front of the rest of the squad was the girl who'd caught his heart just minutes earlier.

That was a quick change of clothes, Devon thought. Had he been daydreaming longer than he realized? Was there a secret changing room for cheerleaders under the bleachers?

The girl finished up the cheer by executing a series of high jumps. Her cheeks were bright, and he could practically feel the energy radiating from her body.

Who cares how she changed into her uniform so quickly? he thought. All he cared about was that now he'd be able to watch her throughout the game. What a heavenly thought. Still, he had to admit that he liked the pale yellow dress more than the cheerleading uniform. He stared at her smiling face as she launched into another cheer, and then Devon's mind started to drift.

He imagined it was his first day of classes at Sweet Valley High. He didn't know anyone in school, but all day long he kept seeing that blond girl. She was wearing that same sundress, and every time he looked her way, he'd see her looking back at him and smiling.

Devon let himself dive further into the fantasy. The girl was in his last class. After the final bell the two of them lingered until there was no one else in the room. Then, just as she was about to leave, Devon stepped in front of her. "Wait," he'd say. "I think we should talk."

The girl wouldn't say anything for a moment. She had just a hint of shyness about her. Then she'd look at him from under her long lashes and say, "I've been hoping you'd come to me."

Then he'd walk the girl to her locker, but they wouldn't talk very much. They wouldn't need to.

The electricity between them would say everything they needed to know.

They'd make a date for that night. He'd pick her up at her house. Then she'd sit behind him on his motorcycle and clasp her hands tightly around his waist. He'd feel the softness of her body pressed against him and feel her breath on his ear. They'd roar off into the night, the skirt of her pale yellow dress whipping behind her.

The fans roared, and Devon was shaken out of his daydream. He watched his dream girl as she led the rest of the team in a quick dance combination.

"You don't know who I am," Devon said quietly, "but you will be mine."

Lila took Steven's hand as they left the school building.

"Just being friendly," she said with a wink that held a hint of flirtation—only a hint.

"Maybe we aren't being quite friendly enough," Steven said as he slipped an arm around her shoulders.

"I can't wait to see Jessica's face—and Elizabeth's— when they see us together," Lila said with a laugh.

"They're going to go *ballistic*," Steven said. "It'll drive them absolutely crazy to think their nasty little plan backfired. It's perfect." He began leaning closer to Lila. "Maybe we should even kiss," he said with a mischievous twinkle in his eye.

Lila pushed him away playfully. Suddenly her heart clenched, and the smile vanished from her face.

"Oh, Steven," she breathed hoarsely, backing away from him. She felt the color drain from her face, and her whole body trembled. "It's *him.*"

Steven froze. Lila saw an uncomprehending look come over his face. "It's John Pfeifer," she whispered, nodding toward the bushes at the side of the building. "He's following us."

No sooner were the words out of her mouth than there was a rustling in the bushes. John turned and bolted.

"You go to the bleachers," Steven told Lila in a low voice. "I'm going to turn the tables and follow *him.*" He whirled around and took off after John, who was rounding the side of the building.

"Hold it, Pfeifer!" Steven yelled as he ran. John didn't even flinch.

A white-hot flash of rage surged through Lila's veins. She was tired of being afraid of John Pfeifer, tired of looking over her shoulder every five minutes. It was time to confront him. Lila ran after Steven.

Her heart pounded in her chest from nervousness, and her lungs felt hot—as if they were about to burst from the effort of keeping up with Steven and John.

As she rounded the side of the school after them, she had a knife-edged stab of intuition that John had been planning something horrible—and that there was something darker and more terrifying lurking inside him than she could possibly imagine.

Lila saw John's athletic form up ahead, clad in white jeans, sneakers, and a striped shirt. Suddenly Steven lurched forward and tackled John to the asphalt. There was a horrible scraping sound, and Lila stopped and let out a squeal. The two boys scuffled for a moment, but then John kicked Steven away and wrestled himself free. It took a moment for Steven to get back on his feet. John glanced over his shoulder once and took off again, heading around the front of the gym.

"Don't let him get away!" Lila yelled. Steven finally stood and ran after John, but his pace was slower this time. Lila was able to catch up to him, and she jogged along at his side.

"Where did he go?" Steven asked between gasps.

"Around the front," Lila answered with effort. "We can't let him get to the parking lot."

"If he gets away, we'll never prove he was spying on us!" Steven managed. Grabbing her hand, he pulled her around the corner.

Lila looked up and skidded to a stop. John Pfeifer was standing less than three yards away.

Lila stifled a gasp. John's eyes were wild and red. Sweat poured from his temples down his face, and his shirt clung to his body. He was shaking violently, and his back was pinned up against the gym wall. His hands were clasped behind him.

"Don't come any closer!" John screamed.

"Calm down, John." Steven spoke in a firm voice. He took a step toward him.

"Stop right there, Wakefield," John hissed. His eyes darted around as if he had no control over them.

Then suddenly John focused his gaze on Lila. His eyes seemed to bore through her. She lifted her chin and forced herself to return his stare. Lila shuddered at the look in his eyes. They were a terrifying swirl of hatred, darkness, and insanity. She had seen that look once before—the night he had tried to rape her.

John shifted his gaze to Steven, and Lila's knees went weak with relief. She couldn't have kept up her false courage much longer.

"You're the real take-charge type, aren't you?" John said to Steven. His lips curled into a grim smile. "Well, you're through giving orders. I'm in charge now."

Lila gasped as John turned slightly to show them what he had been holding behind his back. She realized immediately that it was a bomb—and not just a soda can bomb either. The thing was huge, made from a thick piece of pipe. Fragments of rags and a short fuse protruded from one end.

Lila felt as if all the wind had been knocked out of her. If Steven hadn't grabbed her and pulled her backward, she didn't think she would have been capable of moving.

I knew it, Lila thought. *He's completely psycho.*

"Don't do anything foolish," Steven said quietly.

"Foolish," John echoed. An eerie laugh erupted from his lips. Then he turned to Lila, his face full of fury.

"You're the one who did something foolish, Lila," he growled. "I cared for you. All I wanted was for you to love me. Instead you destroyed me. After you told everyone I tried to rape you, I was an outcast. And it was a lie!" His voice rose steadily until he.was shrieking.

"No, it wasn't a lie," Lila said in a choked voice. "I wish it wasn't the truth, but it was. You attacked me."

"Shut up!" The rage in John's face seemed to explode. Lila did as she was told.

"I'll always be an outcast because of you," he said. Suddenly a sly expression slid over his features.

"You thought I wasn't good enough for the rich, popular, beautiful Miss Lila Fowler," he said with a twisted smile. "You treated me like the dirt under your feet."

"I didn't mean to, John," Lila said pleadingly. "I was afraid of you, that's all. Just afraid."

John went on rambling insanely, as if he hadn't heard a word she'd said. "You treated me like garbage, and you thought you had beaten me, but you were wrong. I figured out a way to get back at you." The psychotic laughter bubbled from his lips again.

"Look, John," Steven said, inching backward and pulling Lila along. "Let's just talk this out."

"It wasn't easy," John continued. "But I made up my mind that since you had destroyed my life, I was going to destroy yours. And I'm a lot smarter than you think, Lila. I'm a lot smarter than anyone thinks."

John was staring into space now. Lila cast a frightened look at Steven. She could see that the wheels were turning in his mind as he tried frantically to figure a way out of this. They continued to inch backward.

"Why don't we run?" Lila hissed.

"If we make a move, it might set him off," Steven whispered. "There's no way we could get far enough away fast enough."

Lila bit her lip to keep from whimpering as Steven's words sank in. If they couldn't get away fast enough by running, this creeping backward thing certainly wasn't going to help. *I don't want to die,* Lila wailed inwardly.

"Not only did I burn Fowler Crest," John was saying. "I made everyone think you did it, Lila." Suddenly John fixed her with his insane gaze. "How does it feel to be an outcast?" he snarled.

Lila remained silent. It was clear that John wasn't looking for an answer. He merely wanted to taunt her. He was enjoying himself.

John's features went slack, as if he were an electric

doll and someone had pulled the plug. He spoke as if he were in a trance.

"I never would have imagined that I'd find fire so fascinating," he breathed. "The wildness . . . the color . . . the power of it. When I saw Fowler Crest go up in flames, I felt ten feet tall. I felt as if I was holding the world in the palms of my hands. And then when I saw the explosion in the restaurant . . . for the first time in my life I knew what it was like to feel really *alive*."

John looked at Lila. His eyes were flat, like two coins resting on the surface of his face. The emptiness she saw there was more frightening than the twisted rage she had glimpsed before. There would be no reasoning with him, she realized.

"I'm going to go out in a blaze of glory, Lila. And I'm going to take you with me." He glanced at Steven. "I guess you'll be coming along too."

The next few moments seemed to happen in slow motion. Lila watched John light the fuse, then turn and raise the hand that held the bomb.

"Lila, run!" Steven yelled. He launched himself forward, leaping toward John. He was too late. At the same time John pulled his arm back and hurled the flaming bomb into the air.

Lila watched the thing arc ever so gracefully. The sound of breaking glass shattered the stillness as the bomb crashed through a window.

Then there was a moment of silence.

Steven grabbed Lila by the arm and yelled, "Now!"

Lila's feet had already started to fly over the ground. She took a single look back over her shoulder, and her blood ran cold. John was standing perfectly still, grinning like a maniac as tears streamed down his face. He clenched his fists and screamed at the top of his lungs.

"Alive!"

Chapter 11

Elizabeth smiled up at Todd as they walked toward the bleachers. She had just settled in with him for the second half when he had decided he was starving and dragged her back over to the concession stand. Now they were making their way back, and Todd's arms were loaded down with snacks.

"Are you sure you can handle all that food?" she asked with a laugh.

"Sure." Todd smiled. He was balancing a cardboard tray loaded with sodas, hot dogs, potato chips, and peanuts. Elizabeth had figured Steven would be joining them in the bleachers—without Lila—so they had bought a few extra things for him.

Todd leaned over and planted a kiss on Elizabeth's forehead. As he did, the side of the cardboard tray holding the three sodas dipped to one side. He tried to sidestep to balance everything, but it was useless. The sodas splashed to the ground, and the rest of the snacks followed. A moment later Todd was standing there with a foolish look on his face and a single bag of potato chips in his hand.

Elizabeth burst out laughing. "You should see your face," she said. "It's like, 'How in the world did this happen to me?'"

Todd reddened a little. "It only happened because I kissed you," he said with a grin. "Oh, well. I guess I'm stuck with springing for some more food." He turned back to the snack bar. "C'mon."

"Wait." Elizabeth stiffened. She couldn't explain it, but suddenly she felt as if every nerve in her body was on alert . . . electrified.

"What's the matter?" Todd asked. He reached forward and took her hand. "Liz! You're ice cold!"

"Something is very wrong," Elizabeth said in a shaky voice. She could actually feel the skin on her scalp tightening with fear. The blood pounded in her head.

"Jessica?" Todd asked.

Elizabeth swallowed and glanced at the cheerleaders. Jessica was staring back at her, her eyes wide with fear. A sinking feeling of dread hit Elizabeth like a sledgehammer.

"Steven," she whispered.

A fraction of a second later her world erupted

163

in chaos. Elizabeth heard a hissing sound, followed by what sounded like the deafening roar of some terrifying beast.

The sound seemed to reach out and pull everyone inside it. Then Elizabeth watched in horror as the gymnasium blew out, sending flying glass spewing into the air.

The earth seemed to tilt under her feet as the force of the explosion sent shock waves out onto the football field. Todd grabbed her up in his arms and shielded her face. Elizabeth squeezed her eyes shut and clutched at Todd's shoulders. When she looked up a second later, flames were exploding from what was left of the gym.

"No!" Elizabeth shrieked. "Steven is inside!" She pulled herself out of Todd's arms and began racing toward the school building.

"Elizabeth, wait! Don't go near there!" Todd cried, but she paid no attention.

If anything happens to Steven and Lila, it's our fault—Jessica's and mine, Elizabeth thought frantically. All around her people were running, sobbing, and screaming, but all she could think about was her brother.

The closer Elizabeth got to the school, the thicker the crowd became. People were thundering off the bleachers. A few were trying to find out what had happened, but most were trying to get away.

A handful of people had managed to reach the parking lot. In their confusion they had only succeeded in boxing each other in. They seesawed the cars back and forth uselessly, all the while leaning on their horns.

Meanwhile Elizabeth threaded her way through the glut of bodies near the opening in the fence that surrounded the field, mindlessly pushing, shoving, and elbowing aside anyone who stood in her way.

"Let me through! Let me through!" she cried, sobbing hysterically.

"Liz! Wait up!" Elizabeth heard Todd calling to her from somewhere nearby, but she didn't have time to turn around and find him.

Panic was turning the crowd into a stampeding herd. Security guards raced amid the chaotic throng, attempting to control the crowd with flares and bullhorns.

Elizabeth streaked between two guards and charged toward the burning building.

"Stop, miss!" a guard called after her, but Elizabeth barely heard him. She raced ahead toward the leaping flames.

The guard ran after her and grabbed her by both arms. "Let me go!" she yelled, struggling. "My brother is inside!"

She was being dragged backward. "You can't help him. You'll only get hurt yourself," the guard said.

"Elizabeth!" a voice called.

At the sound of her name Elizabeth stopped struggling for a moment. Her eyes searched the crowd.

"Elizabeth!"

Jessica was standing at the edge of the crowd, looking as if she was about to faint. Tears were streaming down her cheeks.

Jessica held out her arms, and Elizabeth ran into them. In a moment Todd was at their side, trying to soothe their nerves.

"I'm sure Steven's fine," Todd said quietly. "Just try not to panic."

But Elizabeth only sobbed harder. *It's our fault,* she told herself again. *If we hadn't been so selfish, Steven and Lila would be with us right now.*

Soon the shrill sound of fire engine alarms and police sirens filled the air. Elizabeth raised her head. Through bleary eyes she watched firefighters jump from the arriving trucks. They flew into a frenzy of activity, unraveling fire hoses and swarming around the building.

By then the ambulances had pulled up, their haunting wail announcing their arrival.

A line of police cars screeched to a stop and uniformed officers sprang into action, organizing the crowd and quieting hysterical bystanders. An older officer with her gray hair pulled back in a bun rolled out yellow tape to keep the crowd at bay.

The sounds of panic and hysteria were gradually

dying down, giving way to quiet sobbing and murmured questions. Everyone stood there, staring at the school . . . waiting.

Then suddenly a buzz of excitement went through the throng of people as a few firemen rounded the corner of the building. They were leading two staggering figures wrapped in blankets. Elizabeth's heart leaped.

"It's Steven and Lila!" she cried, lurching forward. A guard immediately grabbed her and held her back.

"Please find out if they're OK," Elizabeth heard Jessica plead. "It's my brother and a friend."

The guard nodded. "All right. But wait here." Elizabeth held her breath as the guard consulted with an emergency worker who was leading Lila toward the back of an ambulance. Steven was already sitting on the bumper. The guard nodded and then began weaving his way back through the crowd of firefighters and cops.

"As nearly as anyone can tell, your brother and the girl will be OK," he said. "They have some cuts and bruises, and they need some attention, but there are no broken bones."

Elizabeth let out a long, slow breath. "Can we see them?" she asked hopefully.

"Sorry, miss," the guard answered. "They don't want to let anyone through until they're sure the fire is contained. The police also want to question your brother and the girl to find out if they saw anything,

167

but they should be able to go home in a few hours."

"Thank you," Elizabeth said. The guard smiled and walked away. Jessica clasped Elizabeth's hand.

"I don't think I could have lived with myself if anything had happened to them," she said.

"Neither could I," Elizabeth whispered as tears spilled from her eyes.

Suddenly a hush fell over the crowd. Two firemen, their faces red and covered with a layer of sweat and soot, were carrying a stretcher toward an ambulance. On it was a body, completely covered in a dark blanket from head to foot.

A horrified murmur broke the silence and swept through the crowd like a wave. Everyone realized what the blanket meant.

Dead.

Elizabeth felt the heightened tension as everyone around her held their breath, silently asking the same question. *Who is it?*

Lila stood with her back to the ambulance, her face illuminated by the flashing lights on the fire trucks, police cars, and ambulances. She shivered in the warm afternoon air in spite of the blanket wrapped around her.

There was a gash on her forehead, and her arms were covered with tiny cuts made by flying glass. Both legs were bruised, and her knees were bloody from when she had been propelled to the ground by the force of the explosion. Her designer dress was now a torn, muddy rag.

Silent tears rolled down Lila's cheeks, the result of a mixture of shock and relief. As she looked at the scene before her Lila didn't even realize she was crying.

Soot and cinders whirled in the air. Firefighters and police and ambulance workers were everywhere—moving equipment and shouting orders, barking into walkie-talkies, or just standing by.

Steven stood at her side, his hand on her shoulder. She was glad for his presence. His strength gave her strength.

She looked up at him. "I can't believe I'm alive," she said through dry parched lips. "I'm afraid I'll find out I'm in one of those horror stories where the character is dead but doesn't know it yet." A single dry sob shook her body. "It's all so terrible—like a horrible, horrible dream. Except I'll never wake up."

"Shhh, shhh," Steven said gently. He took her in his arms and ran his hand over her hair. "You're alive, and you'll live through this. You'll have your old life back, and it's a wonderful life, Lila. It's a life most girls would envy."

Lila attempted a smile and failed. "I suppose so," she said. "But I wish people *didn't* envy me. They only do because they don't know that my life isn't as perfect as they think. After all, look at this." She gestured to the scene around them. "All this happened because of me." A chill shot through her, and her teeth began chattering.

"Don't blame yourself, Lila," Steven said. "All of this happened because of *John*." He drew her blanket tighter around her.

"John," Lila whispered. A moment later she realized something had changed—the crowd had fallen silent. She looked around quickly. "What is it?"

Then Lila saw the stretcher. She felt a wave of nausea and grabbed Steven for support.

"I'll go check it out," Steven said quietly. He helped Lila to a seat in the back of the ambulance, then walked over to speak with a police officer standing near the body.

When he returned, Lila saw that his face was ashen. Lila stood shakily, her heard thudding in her chest.

"It's John Pfeifer, Lila," Steven told her. "He's dead."

"I knew it," Lila said softly. "There was no way he could have survived that blast." She looked up at Steven with wide, frightened eyes. "Do you remember the last word he said? It was *alive*." Without warning, uncontrollable sobs burst forth, leaving Lila gasping for breath.

As the tears streamed down her cheeks Lila saw an

EMS worker in a white coat approaching. "Excuse me, miss," she said, putting a hand on Lila's arm. "You seem to be very upset. Why don't you step into the ambulance and I'll give you something to help you calm down."

Lila pulled away from her. "Leave me alone!" she shrieked. "Don't you dare come near me!"

Lila felt herself spinning out of control as images flew through her mind. John's smiling face when she first agreed to go out with him, his steely glare that night at Miller's Point when he tried to rape her, the psychotic look in his eyes as he screamed his final word . . . *alive*.

The EMS worker backed away as Lila paced, shaking her head to try to clear her thoughts. Lila was dimly aware of Steven's voice, telling her to calm down. To listen to him.

Finally Steven grabbed her by the shoulders, forcing her to stop walking. Lila looked into Steven's kind, concerned eyes as he murmured soothing words.

Over his shoulder she caught a glimpse of Elizabeth and Jessica, staring at her with red, swollen eyes. Then Steven folded her in his arms, and she buried her head against his chest and cried.

Chapter 12

The following morning Steven stood in the kitchen wearing his robe and pajamas, cooking up a pancake breakfast. He was glad to be performing such a normal task. The past twenty-four hours had been a blur.

Steven ladled some batter onto the steaming griddle and smiled. After Lila had had her little breakdown, she had totally surprised Steven.

Lila had seemed to draw from a well of strength. In scarcely a minute she had changed from a babbling and terrified young girl into a calm and resigned young woman.

A sigh escaped Steven's lips. It had been a long night. They had both been examined, treated, and questioned extensively by the police. By the time he and Lila got home, it was nearly two in the morning. Lila had spent the night at the Wakefields', and

Steven's worried parents had questioned them both for another hour and a half before they were finally allowed to go to sleep.

"And still I'm the first one up," Steven said aloud, chuckling to himself. He flipped a couple of pancakes onto a platter and placed them in the oven to keep them warm. When he looked up, Jessica and Elizabeth were shuffling sleepily into the kitchen.

Jessica's hair was sticking out in all directions, and she was wearing a new silk robe. Elizabeth wore one of her old favorites, a fuzzy pink flannel with yellow roses, and her hair was pulled back neatly in a low ponytail. *Even tragedy can't change some things,* Steven thought with a wry smile.

Jessica sniffed the air. "Mmm, pancakes. I *love* having you home, Steven," she said as she took a seat. She scraped her chair backward on the floor.

"Quiet!" Steven protested. "I don't want to wake Mom and Dad. They'll start asking me questions about the accident all over again."

"OK, OK. I'm sorry," Jessica said.

"Where's Lila?" Steven asked.

"She's still sleeping," Jessica said with a yawn.

"I think she really needs the rest," Elizabeth added, helping herself to some orange juice.

"That's an understatement," Steven said as he placed the pancake platter in the center of the table.

"I still can't believe the whole gym exploded!"

Jessica said, reaching forward to grab some steaming pancakes.

"I can't believe John Pfeifer is dead," Elizabeth said seriously. She nibbled on a piece of bacon.

"Good riddance!" Jessica said loudly.

"Jessica!" Elizabeth hissed.

"Oh, don't get all high-and-mighty on me, Liz," Jessica shot back. "The guy tried to rape two girls, destroyed Lila's house, and tried to kill our own brother. Are you going to tell me he didn't deserve what he got?"

Elizabeth opened her mouth to respond, but Steven felt the need to stop the conversation before it started.

"Can we please talk about something else?" he asked, taking a seat and picking up his coffee cup.

He watched Elizabeth and Jessica shoot each other annoyed glances, but then Elizabeth turned to him.

"So what are you going to do now?" she asked. "Will you be going back to school soon?"

Steven smiled. He knew his sisters wanted him back at SVU and as far away from Lila Fowler as possible. But he wasn't going to flee just yet. Not until his lovely twin sisters got the shock of the century.

"What are you grinning about, Steven?" Elizabeth asked. "You look like the cat that just caught the mouse."

Steven gave her a look of wide-eyed innocence. "Really? I don't know what you mean!"

The doorbell rang and Steven jumped up, happy to avoid any further questions about his future.

Steven hurried to the door and swung it open. When he saw the figure standing on the front step, his jaw dropped.

"Mister . . . uh, Mr. Garrison," Steven stuttered.

The tough-looking D.A. was dressed in his trademark charcoal gray suit and carried his black leather briefcase. His keen blue eyes usually maintained a steady gaze, but now they flickered over Steven's face. The D.A. cleared his throat. "May I come in?"

"Uh . . . of course!" Steven said hurriedly. He practically jumped aside to let the D.A. pass.

"I really wasn't expecting any visitors," Steven said. He felt foolish, standing there in front of the D.A. wearing his robe and pajamas.

"Don't worry about it," Garrison said gruffly. He started to sit down on the sofa, then spotted a straight-backed chair and chose that instead. "Please have a seat," he told Steven.

"Thanks," Steven replied, sinking onto the sofa. He felt strange being asked to have a seat in his own house. Then he decided that coming from Joe Garrison, it was almost normal. The D.A. had grown used to giving orders out of habit—and most people, including Steven, had grown used to taking them.

"Can I get you some coffee or tea?" Steven asked.

Garrison shook his head. "No, thank you. I'd like to get right to the point. I'm offering you your internship back. Do you want it?"

Suddenly Steven's legs felt like jelly. He sank onto the sofa. "You're asking me if I'll accept it?" he whispered. "Of course I will."

As soon as the words were out of his mouth the twins came bounding into the room.

"Congratulations, Steven!" Elizabeth cried, giving him a big hug.

"This is fantastic!" Jessica shrieked. She hugged him too. Then she startled the D.A. by planting a kiss on his cheek.

"Sorry," she said when he reddened. "I'm just so happy that I can't help myself."

For once the D.A. seemed at a loss for words.

"Sit down and keep still, you two," Steven told the twins. He knew if they kept acting so giddy, he'd be bouncing up and down along with them, and he wanted to maintain a bit of dignity. Steven turned to Garrison.

"What made you change your mind?" he asked.

The D.A. cleared his throat. When he spoke, his gravelly voice had a humble note in it. "In light of what happened with John Pfeifer, I've decided that your feelings about Miss Fowler's innocence weren't based on your personal involvement with her after all."

Steven's heart soared in triumph, and he had to use every ounce of his strength to keep from grinning.

"What I'm saying is that I realize I was unfair to you, and I . . . I apologize," the D.A. said. "You made some pretty smart deductions."

Steven felt strangely off-balance. He had never heard the D.A. admit he was wrong.

"That John Pfeifer was like a ticking time bomb," the D.A. explained, shifting in his seat. "Our boys found all sorts of incriminating evidence in his room. He had been stalking Miss Fowler for nearly a year—even kept a diary about it. In it were notes on her schedule and pages of hateful rumblings about how he'd get even with her for destroying his life. He also had tons of information on constructing bombs."

"I knew it!" Steven exclaimed before he realized what he was saying. He cleared his throat and tried to sound professional. "I mean, I knew that if we got a look at his room, we'd find something."

"Well, you were right there too, Steven," the D.A. said, looking down at the floor for a split second. Steven thought the man almost looked humble. "That diary confirmed every one of your theories. He even recorded the day he downloaded that information from the Web and planted it on your desk. And he stole Miss Fowler's monogrammed gloves months ago. It seems he'd been planning this for a long time."

Steven looked at his sisters. He could tell they were

as overcome by the news as he was. They had been going to school on a daily basis with a violent psychotic.

The D.A. got to his feet. "I should be going, Wakefield," he said, wiping his hands on his slacks. He grabbed his briefcase and squared his shoulders. "The case against Miss Fowler is being dismissed. Good-bye, Steven. Good morning, ladies." He started across the room. Steven walked over quickly and opened the door for his boss.

Garrison gave Steven a quick nod and left.

When the D.A. was gone, the twins jumped up and hugged Steven again.

"You must be so psyched!" Jessica bubbled.

"Maybe you should call Billie and tell her all about it," Elizabeth added.

"What's going on?"

Steven turned to find Lila standing at the bottom of the steps, rubbing her eyes. She was wearing one of Jessica's white silk nightgowns. *Perfect,* Steven thought.

"Lila, darling," he said, grabbing her hand and giving her a secret wink. "I have great news. I just got my job back."

Lila blinked groggily, obviously still half asleep. Then realization swept over her face, and she winked back at Steven.

"Oh, my love muffin! That's fabulous!" she cooed, grasping his arm. "Don't you think it's the perfect time to tell them our other incredible news?"

Steven grinned. Lila's performance was inspired. He looked back at his sisters, who were both gaping at him.

"Hold on to your hats, kids!" Steven said. "Lila and I are engaged!"

Lila threw her arms around Steven's neck, and Steven caught a glimpse of his sisters grabbing on to each other for support. *You're not the only Wakefields who can scheme, dear sisters.*

"Home, sweet home!" Lila said as Steven pulled the VW to a stop in front of Fowler Crest. There was a note of false gaiety in her voice.

I should be happy that this whole thing is over, she said to herself. *I'm cleared, Steven has his job back, and Jessica and Elizabeth got what they deserved.* But inside, Lila felt lost. She turned to Steven, determined to keep her feelings hidden.

"I think we've given your sisters plenty to think about," she said. "Poor Jessica probably won't be able to eat for a week. Did you see how positively green she turned? And I'll never forget the look on Elizabeth's face when she ran from the room."

Steven dissolved into laughter. "It was a pretty good trick," he said. "It serves the two of them right for meddling in our lives. They'll remember this lesson for a long, long time."

Lila tucked a loose strand of hair behind her ear and smoothed the pink skirt she had "borrowed" from Jessica's closet. She couldn't have asked Jessica's permission because it looked like her so-called best friend wasn't speaking to her again.

"I can't wait until they find out they've been tricked," she said. Then she paused and glanced at the house. Ironically the construction had been completed the afternoon before. While John had been busy destroying the school, the crew here had been packing it in. "Oh, well. I guess I'd better go," Lila said.

Steven put a hand on her arm. "Not so fast. Is something the matter? You seem a little down all of a sudden."

Lila's lip quivered. "I should have known I couldn't hide it from you," she said. She twisted her hands in her lap. "I don't know what's the matter with me. The whole ordeal is over, and all the charges have been dropped. You'd think I'd be jumping for joy."

Lila looked out the car window. "The repairs are done. The furniture will have to be replaced, but otherwise no one would ever suspect there had been a fire." She turned back to Steven. "I just feel lost, and I don't know why."

Steven put his hand over hers. "You've been through a lot, Lila. Many people would be in worse shape than you, but you're strong. I'm sure of it. You'll get over this. You just need some time to regroup, and then you'll bounce back."

Lila let the words sink in. She had come to value Steven's opinion tremendously. "I hope it happens soon," she said. She looked into his eyes. "I don't know what I would have done without you, Steven. Thanks for believing in me."

Steven gave her a half smile. "Anytime, pal." He ran his hand along the steering wheel. "Let's keep in touch. Maybe get together for a burger sometime," he said with a wink.

Lila chuckled. "Or maybe some champagne and caviar," she said as she opened the car door. As she got out she returned Steven's wink. "I'll be seeing you," she said softly.

I'm feeling a little lost myself, Steven realized after he dropped Lila off. For the past several weeks he had put all his energy into solving the Fowler Crest case and into his romance with Lila. Now that the case was pretty well wrapped up and he and Lila were no longer an item, he felt at loose ends.

As he drove around aimlessly he noticed that the sky was darkening and storm clouds were beginning to gather. *The weather is beginning to match my mood,* he thought.

He knew there must be something he could do to cheer himself up, but he couldn't figure out what it was. Then, out of nowhere, Elizabeth's voice floated through his mind. *Maybe you should call Billie and tell her all about it.* Suddenly Steven knew exactly where he wanted to go and exactly what he needed to do.

Five minutes later he was pulling into a parking spot in front of the courthouse. He practically ran inside the building. Then he paced impatiently in front of the elevator.

His heart pounded as he opened the door to the D.A.'s offices. As usual the place was a buzz of activity, even on the weekend. When he walked inside, he was greeted with welcoming smiles.

Steven returned the greetings and then headed for his old cubicle. It felt great to sit down behind his desk again. For a moment he just sat there, his fingers laced behind his head, savoring his victory.

His mind drifted back to the day the D.A. had dismissed him. He remembered how forlorn he had felt saying good-bye to everyone and getting his things together. Then in slow motion he saw Billie's picture in his mind's eye as it fell from a notebook . . . her smiling face . . . her twinkling eyes.

Steven's hands trembled slightly as he reached for the phone and dialed Billie's number. Would she talk to him? What if she didn't want anything to do with him? What if she had a new boyfriend? Steven's heart hardened at the thought. He gripped the phone with a sweaty hand.

The line rang once, twice, three times. *Be*

there, Steven pleaded. He *had* to talk to her.

"Hello?" Billie answered breathlessly after the fifth ring.

"Hi, uh, Billie. It's me, Steven." He held his breath.

"Hi, Steven," Billie said coolly.

"It's so good to hear your voice," Steven said softly. There was a pause.

"It's good to hear yours too," she said finally. Warmth surged through Steven. He could almost see her, the phone pressed against her ear underneath a tangle of chestnut curls. Somehow he knew that things would be all right between them.

"Billie, I've missed you," he said.

"I've missed you too, Steven."

Chapter 13

After Steven had gone, Lila strolled around the grounds of Fowler Crest. A warm breeze caressed her skin, but she felt a cold, hollow emptiness inside. She hated the idea of going indoors and being by herself in the huge mansion once more.

After a while Lila sat down on the steps and hugged her knees to her chest. She felt a pang of regret that things hadn't worked out with Steven. He was a good person, and she admired him in many ways. He had stood by her through the worst ordeal of her life, and when she'd said she couldn't have gotten through it without him, she'd meant it.

She wrinkled her nose. Nevertheless, Jessica and Elizabeth were right. Trying to have a relationship with Steven would be as impossible as mixing oil and water.

She wished it could be otherwise. Then she wouldn't feel so all alone.

She sighed. *Stop feeling sorry for yourself,* a voice in her brain scolded. Lila pulled herself to her feet.

"What I need is a long bubble bath," she said with determination. She turned and pushed through the front door.

Once inside the mansion, however, Lila wasn't so sure. The house was so big, and so empty. The thought that she would sleep there alone again that night sent her heart plummeting down to her ankles. Then she heard voices.

Lila did a double take as she saw her mother hurrying down the staircase toward her. She was still dressed in the linen suit and pillbox hat she favored for traveling. There was a pained expression on her face.

"Oh, dear, it's so good to see you! We've been frantic!" she gushed, sweeping Lila into her arms.

Mr. Fowler wasn't far behind. "I'm so glad that you're all right," he said in a choked voice. Lila freed herself gently from her mother's embrace and stared at her father in astonishment. His normally ruddy face had gone pale. She had never seen him look so shaken.

She felt a rush of feeling as she realized she had underestimated how much her parents cared for her. This unexpected outpouring of emotion from them left her totally off-balance.

"When did you guys get in?" Lila asked, finding her voice.

"Oh, a little over an hour ago. I guess we didn't hear you drive up," Lila's father said. Then he reached out and clasped her hand. "I was so worried, honey," he said.

"We stopped at Carter's Drugstore on the way home," he explained. "Mr. Carter filled us in on what's been going on while we were away. I'm so sorry we weren't here, Lila."

Tears welled up in Lila's eyes, but she blinked them back. She didn't want to cry any more.

"It's a horror!" her mother cried, stroking Lila's hair. "When I heard there was a fire while you were here all alone, well, I thought I would faint on the spot," she wailed.

"And when I heard that you'd been arrested, I was infuriated," her father thundered. He shook his fist in the air. "How dare they treat my daughter like a criminal? To think of how humiliated, how terrified you must have been . . ."

Lila could see her father working himself up into one of his famous rages. His face was beet red.

"When I think that I'm paying taxes for such slipshod police work, I . . . I . . ." Mr. Fowler shook his head. "Don't worry, honey. I'm going to see to it that the D.A. makes a public apology to you and that the text appears in the paper."

"You're absolutely right, George." Lila's mother nodded. Her voice was full of indignation. "Lila was horribly treated. And all the while the police should have been protecting her from that parasite, John Pfeifer."

Lila held up her hand for silence. "He won't be bothering me again. He's dead, Mom," she said in a voice barely above a whisper. "I'm just glad he didn't hurt me." She let out a long sigh. "Anyway, it's all over now."

"John Pfeifer—dead?" Mrs. Fowler gasped.

Mr. Fowler's lips were set in a thin line. "That boy was disturbed," he said.

Lila watched as her father clenched and unclenched his jaw. He was obviously trying hard to regain his usual stony composure. She was touched that he was so outraged and upset about what had happened to her. Usually she only saw him carry on so much about business.

Her father turned toward the staircase. "Well, you certainly did a first-rate job of rebuilding the mansion," her father boomed heartily. "I'm proud of you, Lila."

"I'll second that," her mother piped up. "I've always thought you could handle anything that came your way, Lila. This is proof." She gave her daughter's shoulder a quick squeeze.

Lila swallowed. "Thanks for the vote of confidence,

187

both of you. It means a lot to me, but . . ." Her throat suddenly closed up.

"But what, dear?" her mother prompted.

"But . . ." Lila's voice wavered. She took a deep breath. "But it would have meant a lot more to me if I could have heard your voice during the past few weeks, Mom. Yours too, Dad."

Lila took another deep breath. She was dangerously close to crying, and she didn't want to get started. Her parents stared at her in openmouthed silence.

"I felt so alone, so *abandoned*," Lila said in a choked voice. She looked from her mother to her father. "How could the two of you go off to some remote island where you can't be reached? You were gone for nearly a month! And you never even called." Her voice squeaked.

Lila saw her father take her mother's hand. "I had absolutely no idea you felt that way, Lila," he said. "Your mother and I have gone on lots of trips, and you never complained. When I said we'd be unreachable, you should have told me how you felt."

"I didn't think I should have to tell you," Lila said in a small voice. "I may act sophisticated all the time, but I'm still a kid."

Concern and sadness were etched on her mother's face. "I thought you enjoyed your freedom and independence, Lila."

Lila lifted her chin. "I do," she said firmly. "But I still want to know you're there for me. I still want to know you care."

"Of course we care," both of her parents said at the same time.

"We've been selfish and thoughtless," her mother murmured. "It won't happen again. We'll always make sure you have a way to get in touch with us, won't we, George?"

Lila's father nodded solemnly. "We certainly will." He enveloped Lila in a bear hug. She breathed in his familiar cologne and felt truly relieved for the first time in weeks.

"There must be some way we can make it up to you, Lila," her father said after a moment. "What would you say to a new car?"

Lila smiled softly and pulled herself from his arms. "No, thanks, Daddy. I already have a car that I love. You don't have to buy me anything."

"Nonsense," her mother protested. "What about a new Oscar de Roget gown?"

"I really don't need one, Mom. You know, everything doesn't have to be about material possessions."

Lila saw her father's eyebrows shoot up. "What about a diamond tennis bracelet?"

"No, thanks, Dad. Diamonds aren't really my thing anymore."

"Not your thing anymore?" Mrs. Fowler echoed. Her jaw dropped.

Lila chuckled lightly. "Don't get me wrong—I still like them. It's just that they aren't as important to me as they used to be." She shrugged and wrinkled her nose. "I guess I've changed a little."

Mr. Fowler frowned. "If you don't want diamonds, how about that European racing bike you've been admiring?"

"Dad! No, thanks." Lila was really laughing now.

"Ruby earrings?" her mother offered.

Lila threw up her hands. "I told you both that this isn't about material things. You don't have to buy me anything. Can't you tell that I've grown? That I'm different?"

Lila's father pursed his lips. "I see. Well, then, I don't suppose you'd consider an expense-paid ski weekend in Colorado for yourself and a friend, would you?"

Lila had already started to shake her head and stopped abruptly. Aspen was so lovely this time of year. Her lips curved into a smile. "I suppose if it would make you happy, Dad, I could consider it," she said.

Devon knelt on Nana's kitchen floor. He was dressed in what he called his "Mr. Fix-it" outfit— his oldest, most faded jeans worn without a shirt.

As he tightened the screws on the hinge he was replacing on Nana's kitchen cabinet his mind drifted back to the catastrophe at Sweet Valley High the night before. What an introduction to the school!

"There," he whispered as the last screw locked firmly in place. He put down the screwdriver and raked a hand through his hair.

An image of the body being carried away on the stretcher flashed through his mind. *And I thought I had problems.* He shook his head. What kind of life had led that guy to his terrible end?

From the panicked snatches of conversation he'd overheard, he gathered that this guy John had firebombed the school because of an obsession with getting back at a girl named Laura or Lily or something. But he'd also heard that the guy had tried to rape her. He felt a brief shudder of disgust. What a sicko.

Devon wiped a trace of grease on his jeans and began replacing his tools in his toolbox. His mind returned to the girl in the pale yellow dress. He had searched for her during the chaos and confusion, but he hadn't found her.

There was something about that girl that made Devon want to protect her. The more he thought about it, the more certain he was that he had to be with her.

Devon finished putting his tools away and snapped the toolbox shut. *One thing's sure,* he said to himself. *There's more to Sweet Valley than meets the eye. It's not every day that you go to check out your new school and it blows up in your face.*

Nana came bustling into the kitchen. "Oh, Devon, I can't believe you've been working again—and on such a beautiful day!" She patted him on the shoulder. Then she examined the hinge on the cabinet.

"That old thing has been broken for ages," she said. "I kept telling myself I'd get around to fixing it, but I never did."

Devon felt a warm glow. He would have enjoyed helping Nana even if she hadn't expressed so much appreciation for every little thing he did. "No problem," he said. "After all, if this is going to be my new home, I want it to be in good shape."

Nana laughed lightly. "Thanks. Now why don't you get out of the house? You could take a ride down to Sweet Valley Marina. I'll bet it's lovely there now, and I'm sure you'll find some young people around too."

Devon regarded Nana silently for a moment— the kind face with the gentle blue eyes. The past week or so, since he'd been staying with her, she had made him feel more at home than he had ever felt in his life. And she had agreed to be his guardian even though she thought he had been disinherited—cut off without a cent.

It's time to tell her the truth, Devon said to himself. *It's time to tell her about the money.*

Nana was looking at him curiously. "Devon— are you all right?" she asked. "You have the strangest look on your face."

Devon took Nana by the shoulders and steered her toward the kitchen table. "Sit down, Nana," he said firmly. "We've got to talk."

When they were seated across from each other, Devon cleared his throat. "Nana, I haven't been entirely truthful with you."

Nana furrowed her brow. "About what, dear?"

"It's kind of hard for me. I feel so bad about lying to you. . . ." Devon took a deep breath to calm his nerves.

Telling the truth about his money was an even bigger step than he had imagined. It was hard to let go of his mistrust of people now, even though he wanted to. It was kind of like leaping from an airplane without knowing whether you had a para- chute or not.

Nana was still looking at him expectantly. Her hands were folded in the lap of her blue gingham dress. There was a single vertical crease in her forehead above her nose.

"I told you I was broke," Devon said softly. "That I'd been disinherited. It's not true."

Nana unclasped her hands. "I know."

Devon felt as if all the wind had been knocked out of him. The suspicions that had been sleeping deep inside him began to stir. A cautionary voice began whispering to him. *Be careful.*

He looked into Nana's clear blue eyes. Had she been acting all along? Had he been fooled again? He couldn't bear to think so.

"How did you find out?" he asked hoarsely. "How long have you known?"

Nana shook her head. "I spoke too quickly. I didn't know for sure. I simply didn't believe your parents would disinherit you—but when you said they did . . ." Nana let her voice trail off. She rubbed her forehead. "When you told me they did, I thought that maybe it was possible. But it just felt wrong to me."

Devon realized he was sitting on the edge of his chair. He felt lightheaded. "Why was the idea so incredible? I thought it was pretty believable. They hardly even knew I existed. If I *had* been disinherited, I wouldn't have been too surprised."

Nana gave him a long look. "Oh, Devon. I worked for your family for years. When you're around people, you see things." She looked down at her hands for a moment. "Your parents talked about you often."

Devon felt his mouth drop open. He held on to his chair tightly. His parents had hardly seemed to know he was around. "What did they say?" he whispered.

Nana tilted her head back as if she was collecting her thoughts. "One day your father was on his way to some big client meeting. You had played your first Little League game that afternoon."

A sunny smile spread over Nana's face. "Your father was so proud. He told me you outran, outpitched, and outbatted every other kid on the team."

Devon got a faraway look in his eyes. "Strange," he said. "I don't recall him ever coming to a game."

Nana nodded slowly. "Oh, yes. He was so busy with business, but he went whenever he could. You may only remember the bad, Devon, but there was some good mixed in."

"And my mother? What did she have to say?"

Nana paused for a moment. "She often talked about you. One day I was preparing pastries for a tea she was giving. You were going to be there, and you were all dressed up in a little suit. 'Look at my son,' she said. 'He's so smart for his age. He acts like a grown-up already.'"

Devon's eyes misted over, and he wiped a hand across his face. "Why didn't they ever say those things to me?" he whispered. "It would have meant so much."

Nana put a hand on Devon's arm. "That was the problem. They didn't know how to show their love." She pressed her lips into a thin line. "Your mother was jealous of your feelings for me. That's why your parents let me go." Nana stared out the window. "She never said so, of course. But I could feel it."

Devon took another deep breath. He'd have to give this news some time to sink in.

Nana went on speaking. "So when you told me your parents had disinherited you, I found it hard to believe. But then I thought that maybe something had happened during those years I was away from you to change things."

Devon went to the sink and filled a glass with water. His mouth felt dry as dust.

"So now you know about the money," he said. He downed the water in one gulp. "But you don't know how much. It's twenty million dollars."

Devon studied Nana's face closely. He expected amazement, but all he got was a steady stare. "That's a lot of money, Devon," she said. "You should be careful with it. Invest it wisely."

Devon's heart had begun to thaw, and now it warmed further. Nana's reaction was so different from Uncle Mark's and Aunt Peggy's. She didn't care one bit about having the money for herself. She thought only of him.

Nana never ceases to amaze me, he thought. *Even though I know how good she is, she keeps showing me day after day.* He looked away, a little embarrassed at the strength of his emotions.

After a moment Devon sat down and told Nana what had happened with his cousins in Ohio and with his uncle Pete in Las Vegas. When he had finished, Nana's eyes were glistening.

"Oh, Devon, you poor dear," she said softly. "I'd give anything if I could erase the things that happened to you—just wipe them out. But I can't. All I can do is prove to you that everyone isn't like that."

Devon looked into Nana's eyes. "You already have," he said.

After Lila and Steven left, Jessica and Elizabeth sat in the den, slumped on the sofa. An atmosphere of gloom hung in the air, as if the two girls both had black clouds hovering over their heads.

"This engagement is worse for me than it is for you," Jessica told her sister. She hauled herself off the couch and began pacing like a caged animal.

Elizabeth's head snapped up. "Just how do you figure that?" she asked indignantly.

"Easy," Jessica said quickly. "Lila was my best friend. Even though I was mad at her about chasing after Steven, I still hoped we'd be best friends again

197

someday. Now things will never be the same."

"I'm sorry, Jess," Elizabeth said quietly. "I guess I haven't really been thinking of it that way."

"And you know what?" Jessica continued. "Now we really will have to watch them be all lovey-dovey all the time. For the rest of our lives!"

Elizabeth shuddered. "Please don't make me think about it."

"Caroline Pearce will have a field day with this," Jessica said miserably. "Those lips of hers will be flapping a mile a minute. She'll have the news spread all over Sweet Valley High like that." Jessica snapped her fingers. "I won't be able to show my face anywhere. It's so embarrassing."

"Stop worrying so much about what people think," Elizabeth said. She grabbed a magazine off the coffee table but made no move to open it. "What we should be worried about is the fact that Steven is throwing away his life."

"You know I'm worried about that," Jessica said. "But I still hate giving Caroline a single crumb of satisfaction."

Jessica sank onto the couch again. She leaned back and stuck her long legs out in front of her. "Lila and Steven are engaged, and I suppose we just have to accept it," she wailed.

"I can't," Elizabeth said, returning to the table.

"I mean, I can't believe it! He totally belongs with Billie. Why can't he see that?"

"We need a miracle," Jessica said. "Sweet Valley High is not big enough for three Wakefield girls."

"Ugh!" Elizabeth groaned. "Lila Fowler . . . our sister-in-law!"

Ken Matthews always thought Internet chat rooms were for kids with no real friends. Then he accidentally links into an artists' chat room and meets the most amazing girl he's ever known. But when his dream girl asks to meet him in person, Ken panics. Will she dump him when she finds out he's just a stupid jock and not the poet he's been pretending to be? Don't miss the Sweet Valley High Super Romance, **Mystery Date.** *It's the most magical Sweet Valley romance yet!*

When sexy Devon Whitelaw arrives in Sweet Valley, he's going to raise temperatures past the boiling point. He's cool. He's hot. And he'll steal your heart. Don't miss Sweet Valley High #138, **What Jessica Wants. . . .** *Book one in an intense three-part miniseries.*

Bantam Books in the Sweet Valley High series
Ask your bookseller for the books you have missed

SIGN UP FOR THE SWEET VALLEY HIGH® FAN CLUB!

Hey, girls! Get all the gossip on Sweet Valley High's® most popular teenagers when you join our fantastic Fan Club! As a member, you'll get all of this really cool stuff:

- Membership Card with your own personal Fan Club ID number
- A Sweet Valley High® Secret Treasure Box
- Sweet Valley High® Stationery
- Official Fan Club Pencil (for secret note writing!)
- Three Bookmarks
- A "Members Only" Door Hanger
- Two Skeins of J. & P. Coats® Embroidery Floss with flower barrette instruction leaflet
- Two editions of *The Oracle* newsletter
- Plus exclusive Sweet Valley High® product offers, special savings, contests, and much more!

Be the first to find out what Jessica & Elizabeth Wakefield are up to by joining the Sweet Valley High® Fan Club for the one-year membership fee of only $6.25 each for U.S. residents, $8.25 for Canadian residents (U.S. currency). Includes shipping & handling.

Send a check or money order (do not send cash) made payable to "Sweet Valley High® Fan Club" along with this form to:

SWEET VALLEY HIGH® FAN CLUB, BOX 3919-B, SCHAUMBURG, IL 60168-3919

NAME_____
    (Please print clearly)

ADDRESS_____

CITY_____ STATE _____ ZIP_____
                                                       (Required)

AGE_____ BIRTHDAY_____ /_____ /_____